STANDING AGAINST THE WIND

Standing Against the Wind

Traci L. Jones

Farrar, Straus and Giroux
New York

Copyright © 2006 by Traci L. Jones
All rights reserved
Distributed in Canada by Douglas & McIntyre Ltd.
Printed in the United States of America
Designed by Jay Colvin
First edition, 2006
1 3 5 7 9 10 8 6 4 2

www.fsgkidsbooks.com

Library of Congress Cataloging-in-Publication Data
Jones, Traci L.
    Standing against the wind / Traci L. Jones.— 1st ed.
        p. cm.
    Summary: As she tries to escape her poor Chicago neighborhood by
winning a scholarship to a prestigious boarding school, shy and studious
eighth-grader Patrice discovers that she has more options in life than she
previously realized.
    ISBN-13: 978-0-374-37174-6
    ISBN-10: 0-374-37174-1
    [1. Self-confidence—Fiction.   2. Conduct of life—Fiction.
3. Family problems—Fiction.   4. City and town life—Fiction.   5. African
Americans—Fiction.   6. Schools—Fiction.]   I. Title.

PZ7.J72753 Sta 2006
[Fic]—dc22

                                                        2005051226

*For Mom, who thinks everything I do is wonderful,
even when it's not
For Daddy, from whom I get my storytelling
For Peter, for being my brother and my friend,
and especially for marrying Regina
And for Tony, my first, last, and forever true love*

STANDING AGAINST THE WIND

1

MOST DAYS, Patrice Williams really didn't know which she liked least: walking home or actually getting there.

"Just two more blocks," she whispered to herself as she stood waiting for the light.

During the bitterly cold days of winter, the thirteen-year-old had gotten into the habit of counting the blocks until she was safe at home—safe from the freezing cold wind, safe from the nasty comments made by girls who had cut school and were always hanging out in front of the local drugstore, safe from the gang of boys who had all but quit school and who hung out in the broken-down playground in front of her building. They all seemed to have something mean to say about her.

"One more block."

Patrice's quick steps slowed as she noticed the gang of boys from her middle school gathered at the foot of the stairs in front of her building. She had hoped that Chicago's frigid cold would have driven them inside. But even in this weather they were assembled at the only unlocked entrance, attempting to make everyone else's life miserable. They were talking and laughing, looking like teen dragons as the puffs of warm air from their mouths mixed with the clouds of cigarette smoke they blew nonchalantly. Those not smoking blew on their hands and rocked back and forth on their feet, trying to keep warm and look cool at the same time.

The January wind blew directly into Patrice's face. It seemed to reach right through her coat's thin fabric and under her hand-me-down sweatshirt, and pinch her arms with icy, sharp fingers. With the straps of her old backpack long since broken, Patrice's hand felt frozen in a tight fist around its tattered handle. She shivered again, this time more from nervous anticipation than cold.

Trying not to look at the gang of boys, she stopped at the corner to switch the backpack to the other hand. For a brief moment, she wished she had not given her new Christmas gloves to her little cousin. Her old gloves, so worn that the tips of her fingers were poking through holes, were no match against the weather. Clutching her backpack, she scrunched down deeper into her coat to protect her neck from the cold and crossed the street. She shivered again. No matter which direction she walked in, it seemed that the wind blew right in her face, as if to stop her from moving forward.

Patrice was always cold. Her grandmother would have said it was because she was too thin, not enough meat on her bones. Patrice's grandmother used to try and fatten her up with an endless parade of after-school cakes, cookies, and pies.

"Some chocolate cake for my cocoa grandbaby," Grandma would say as she slid an oversized plate of sweets in front of her. And maybe if she had stayed with her paternal grandmother, Patrice wouldn't be a walking stick. But since her mother had spirited her away from her grandmother a little over a year before, her small frame looked as if it hadn't gained one ounce. There was nothing big about Patrice except her large doelike brown eyes and her famous mop of hair.

The only reason Patrice was noticed at Martin Luther King, Jr. Middle School, and in her new neighborhood, was her abundant hair. So aggressive was it that it almost seemed alive. With effort, it could be coaxed into thick braids and ponytails, or even reluctantly convinced to lie in thick, shiny waves that tickled her shoulders. But since there was no one, including Patrice herself, with the time or motivation to coerce her hair into a style, it was usually a big poof that threatened to swallow her head whole. One of her eighth-grade class-mates told Patrice that her hair had all the personality, leaving none for the shy, studious girl who lived under-neath it.

As she got closer to the building, Patrice quickly sur-veyed the group, looking for the only semi-friendly face she could hope to find. She breathed a tiny sigh of relief when she saw Monty Freeman. While Monty wasn't her friend, she knew he wouldn't let the other boys harass her too much. She didn't know what made him cut off their teasing—he never even talked to her—but she was defi-nitely grateful for his sympathy.

Of the five or six boys, there were only three who ever caught her attention. Monty she liked, because of the pity he took on her; Eddie Brooks and Rasheed Walters she despised. They seemed to take pleasure in making her miserable.

Throwing her shoulders back and pretending to be braver than she felt, Patrice picked up her pace and marched toward the steps. She flashed a brief, shy smile at Monty, who returned her acknowledgment with the tiniest, quickest, and, of course, coolest lift of his chin. The other boys smirked at one another and sauntered to the center of the steps, creating a barrier, blocking her ac-cess to the door.

"Hey, Puffy!" sneered Eddie. "When you gonna get that hair of yours done?"

Monty shot a quick neutral glance at Eddie. The other boys snickered, and Patrice's shoulders dropped a bit.

"Yeah, Puffy!" added Rasheed. "Them naps on your head are bad. Ain't your sister still working over at the Cut'n'Style? You need to ask for a family discount."

"Shoot, if her sister is still at the Cut'n'Style, I'll go there myself. She is *too* fine!" hooted Eddie. "Your sister looks good, Puffy. You sure you all got the same mama?"

Patrice threw an angry glare in Eddie's direction and tried to weave her way through the hooting and howling boys, without much success. She didn't know what it was about her that they hated so much, but from the moment she had arrived to live with her aunt they seemed to relish teasing her to tears.

"Leave her alone, fellas," muttered Monty. "As nappy as y'all's heads look, you shouldn't be talking. Let her in."

Heeding their leader's command, the gang of boys cleared a path. Patrice hurried up the stairs and yanked open the door to the building. As it closed slowly behind her, she heard Eddie shout one last nasty comment: "Maybe when your mama get out of jail, she'll comb that head!"

Patrice jabbed the elevator button over and over again, until, through the tears in her eyes, she noticed the OUT OF ORDER sign taped to the door.

With a little whimper, she pulled the stairwell door

open and started up the fifteen flights to her auntie's apartment. At least she would get a chance to stop the tears.

Although the stairwell wasn't exactly what you would call warm, it was better than outside, and the hike up the stairs began to thaw her out. Stopping at the tenth-floor landing, Patrice sat down and tried to compose herself. She knew her auntie Mae would be upset if she came home crying again. Last week she had overheard her aunt talking about her on the phone and it had scared her.

"Yeah, girl, Patrice is a good kid, but she's so tenderhearted. Soft, you know," Auntie Mae had said between puffs on her cigarette. "She smart as a whip in school, but she ain't got *no* street sense. It's hard to believe she's NaNa's daughter. NaNa always had some angle. NaNa's street through and through. Shoot, that's why her fast behind is locked up. But Patrice, she ain't like no kid of mine, or them other kids of NaNa's. Growing up down South with her daddy's mama made her too soft. I don't know if she can make it here or not. Always coming home crying 'bout what them ghetto children be saying to her. When she first got here, they teased her about her accent. Then once she somehow got rid of most of that, it was her hair."

Patrice knew her auntie was right. When she had just arrived, all the kids laughed and mimicked her soft Georgia drawl. Before long she stopped talking to most people, and when she did talk, she tried hard to suppress her accent. She was a shy girl anyway, and the teasing had made her feel worse. Now, even though much of her accent had disappeared, except when she was angry, Patrice was still quiet as a church mouse and twice as shy.

Between puffs on her Newports, her auntie had continued: "Patrice's gotten so quiet. She don't even say nothing back. Just stands there, all hurt. I worry to death about that girl. She may not be able to live here too long. Girl, she can't take it. She ain't got no fight in her. She didn't have much when she got here. Now there ain't no spunk or fire in her at all. This place gonna eat her up. She do help around the house a lot, though. I'll give her that—especially since I had to take on that extra job. I get home and can put my feet up 'cause she done done most of my chores. I'll tell you what, though, my sister was right to take that child to her daddy's mama when she was a baby. Miss Shanice Renée Brown did Patrice a disservice by bringing her up here. She's a sweet girl; I hope she can stay that way."

Patrice shook the memory out of her head and stood up. Auntie Mae was the only one of her mother's five brothers and sisters who'd agreed to take her in, along with her older sister, after her mom got sent to Mount Rose Women's Correctional Center. Her fifteen-year-old half brother, Marquis, had been sentenced to a few years at a juvenile boot camp for trying to rob the local grocery store with a BB gun, so he had a place to stay, at least for the next three years. Patrice and her then seventeen-year-old half sister, Cherise, had almost become wards of the state. So the last thing Patrice wanted to do was make her auntie worry. She might say Patrice was too much trouble to take care of. Auntie Mae worked two jobs and was always so tired. Patrice felt like a burden and went out of her way to help.

She used her still unthawed hands to wipe any trace of tears from her face. Gathering her stuff, she finished hiking the rest of the way to apartment 1525.

Even before opening the door, she could hear the yells coming from inside the apartment.

"It's *my* turn to pick the show!" shouted Nefrititi, Auntie Mae's seven-year-old daughter.

"Is not!" retorted MarcAnthony, her nine-year-old brother. "You were watching that stupid rabbit show when I got home!"

"Hey, guys," Patrice greeted them. "What's the problem now?"

"MarcAnthony won't let me watch my share of TV," whined Nefrititi. "He got to watch two shows yesterday. I should get to watch two shows today."

"Yesterday's all done. Today's a new day!" Marc-Anthony boomed in a deep voice, imitating the preacher at their church.

"Is your homework finished? What about your chores?" asked Patrice, moving the day-old newspapers, half-empty glasses, and overfull ashtrays off the wobbly dining room table and pulling out her schoolwork.

"Yeah," replied MarcAnthony. "It's right there. Mom helped me today." With one hand, he gestured to a pile of paper hanging over the edge of the table, and with the other, he fended off his little sister.

Some cigarette ashes had spilled onto his homework, and he had put a half-empty glass of milk on it as well, leaving a damp circle over problems six and seven. His other schoolwork lay on the floor, scattered under the table. But, despite the mess, the homework was indeed finished.

Patrice sighed. "MarcAnthony, how many times do I have to tell you to put your homework in your backpack when you're done. Where's Auntie Mae? Didn't she walk you home today?"

"Yeah. She just went to the store to get some more cigarettes. Plus, she gotta send a money order to your mama."

Patrice frowned. Mama oughta be sending money to Auntie Mae, not the other way around. Auntie Mae had enough trouble making ends meet since they cut her hours at the factory.

"Why you frowning, Puffy?" asked Nefrititi. "What you mad at?"

"I'm not mad at anything," snapped Patrice. "And stop calling me Puffy. My name is Patrice."

"I know, but everybody at your school calls you Puffy, and them boys downstairs call you Puffy, and your hair's all puffy," Nefrititi rattled off.

"Yeah, so what," Patrice spat. "If everyone jumped out the window, would you be dumb enough to jump, too?"

"I'm sorry." Nefrititi sniffed, apparently contrite. "Don't be mad. I won't ever, ever call you that again. Okay?"

Nefrititi wrapped her skinny arms around Patrice.

"Okay, okay," Patrice said, freeing herself from the too-tight hug. "I'm sorry I snapped at you. I just don't like being called that."

"Then why you let them do it?" asked Nefrititi, putting her little hands on her hips. "I wouldn't let no one call me some stupid name if I didn't like it."

Patrice looked down at her shoes, unwilling to meet her cousin's defiant eyes, and shrugged. "Just don't you call me that, okay?" she muttered.

MarcAnthony, who had been crawling around the floor gathering his homework during this exchange, stood up and looked at Patrice closely. "Well, your hair *is* puffy, but the rest of you is skinny," he observed wisely. "But since you always help me with my homework and stuff, I won't call you Puffy neither. And I'll knock anybody in the head who does, as long as they're not bigger than me."

Patrice smiled, embarrassed that her young cousins had much more nerve than she did. "That won't be necessary, but thank you for the offer, MarcAnthony."

After getting the TV feud settled and cleaning off the dining room table, Patrice sat down and worked diligently on her homework. Unlike other kids in the eighth grade, she liked homework. Since she didn't have any friends, it didn't cut into her social life, and it gave her something to do besides her chores and taking care of MarcAnthony and Nefrititi. She also liked knowing that she had the best grades in class. No matter what the other kids said or what names they called her, they couldn't take that away.

"Aw, man," whined MarcAnthony, looking around the living room for the remote he had hidden from Nefrititi.

"What's the matter now?" asked Patrice, leaning back in her chair to see if the cable had gone out again.

"My show ain't going to be on," he answered. "Some news stuff is on instead."

Patrice shrugged and turned to finish what was left of her homework when she heard the announcer say something that interested her: "*Scholarships are available for outstanding African American students. Dogwood Academy is one of the five predominantly African American boarding schools in the nation. For more—*"

MarcAnthony had dug the remote out of the sofa and clicked off the TV.

"Wait!" shouted Patrice.

"What?" MarcAnthony said.

"That show, turn it back on!"

". . . *and they will send you information about this unique academic opportunity for promising African American scholars, aged thirteen to fifteen.*"

"Darn it!" shouted Patrice. "What show was that?"

MarcAnthony shrugged. "I don't know. It wasn't *Dragon Ball Z*, though."

Patrice didn't know why, but what little she had heard sent sparks shooting through her body. Staring at the blank television, she made a mental note to be sure to get home quicker tomorrow and watch whichever channel it was until she heard that information again. What she had heard sounded, to her, just like hope.

• • •

As Patrice was finishing the last of her homework, Auntie Mae came home, puffing and wheezing from her cold walk to the store and her hike up the stairs with three grocery bags—her hacking and coughing made worse by her two-pack-a-day habit.

Patrice had already started dinner and stood at the stove, stirring Tuna Helper with one hand and holding her assigned reading book with the other.

"Auntie Mae, did you remember to—" started Patrice.

Auntie Mae interrupted her. "Patrice, I saw that boy

Monty in the stairway. He asked me to tell you to stop by his apartment after dinner. Apartment 1010."

Patrice stared at her aunt. Stunned, she stopped stirring. "Monty said what?" she asked incredulously.

Auntie Mae appeared half amused at the open-mouthed, wide-eyed, unbelieving look on her niece's face, and half annoyed at having to repeat herself. "The boy said that he wants you to come by his apartment after dinner. Apartment 1010."

"Why?" asked Patrice, mostly to herself.

"Lord, I don't know." Auntie Mae huffed, taking the spoon from Patrice's hand and stirring the tuna mush. "Anyway, I told him you'd be there 'bout seven-thirty."

"Seven-thirty?" Patrice repeated. "His apartment?"

"Girl, what is your problem? Seven-thirty. His apartment. He probably got to watch them bad kids till his mama get home. Said he would have called you, but they phone got cut off. His mama sure 'nuff is a mess."

"He would have called me?" Patrice muttered.

"Lord Jesus. The boy said he would have, but the phone is cut off! Have mercy. He cute now, but ain't nobody that cute," said Auntie Mae. "This stuff is done; call them kids for dinner."

Patrice barely heard the chatter that was batted back and forth across the Tuna Helper. She hardly ate anyway, but tonight, in a stupor, she ate less than usual, and sat there half dreading, half anticipating the end of the meal.

"You got your homework done?" asked Auntie Mae as Patrice finished clearing the dishes from the dining room table.

"Yes, ma'am," answered Patrice. "Excuse me, Auntie Mae."

Walking down the dim hall to the bathroom, Patrice started feeling a little queasy. She flipped on the light and stared at her image in the mirror. She wasn't too happy about the face that peered back at her.

As she had expected, her hair was, well, puffy. Long overdue for a retouch, there was so much new growth at her scalp that she seemed to have a two-inch Afro connected to the still-straight ends of her hair. She snatched up a brush, massaged in hair oil, and began brushing her hair. After twenty minutes of work, far longer than she ever took with her hair, she managed to create a halfway decent ponytail, one that lay as smoothly against her scalp as her insolent waves would allow.

Patrice pondered whether she should change her clothes or not as she washed her face and brushed her teeth. Deciding against it, she took one final glance in the mirror and shrugged.

"Well, this is as good as it gets, I guess," she said to herself, slamming the brush down.

"Auntie Mae, I'll be back soon to finish the dishes," she called over her shoulder.

Knocking on 1010, Patrice panicked when she heard

a jumble of voices from inside the apartment. What if all Monty's friends were in there? The last thing she wanted to do was deal with them and their smart comments. What could Monty want anyway? Why had she bothered to come? What had she been thinking? Patrice turned to flee back down the hall to the staircase when the door suddenly swung open.

"Hey, you," Monty said casually.

Patrice spun back around and stared at him. "My auntie, she said, you said that I—that you wanted me to come by."

"Yeah. Come in." Monty opened the door fully to reveal the messiest apartment Patrice had ever seen.

Empty fast-food bags were scattered on every surface. Toys covered the floor. Walking past the kitchen, Patrice saw from the corner of her eye dirty plates lying on the counters and stacked in the sink. The room smelled overwhelmingly like a mix of stale cigarette smoke and old fried foods.

Much to Patrice's relief, the voices she'd heard were those of three young boys. At the moment they were hollering at a wrestling match on the big-screen TV, which stood guard over the trash in the living room.

"Dang. Shut up, or I'll turn off the TV," threatened Monty quietly. Miraculously, the boys heard his low voice over their noise, and immediately the yelling quieted to a dull roar of squeaks and exclamations.

"Yeah, um, I need a favor," said Monty, leading Patrice to the back of the apartment toward the bedroom area.

Patrice searched her mind for what this favor could be. She had heard rumors that he sometimes delivered drugs for one of the gangs, although for some reason she didn't really believe he would do that. She was so deep in thought that she bumped into Monty when he stopped in front of a door in the hallway.

As Monty opened a bedroom door, Patrice's heart began to race. She had no idea what favor she could possibly do for Monty, but she was certainly not willing to do anything that involved a bedroom. She was stunned by the number of her classmates here in Chicago who were already pregnant at thirteen or fourteen. It was just one of the many reasons that Patrice knew she would never fit in here.

Apparently seeing her hesitation, Monty looked at her. "Come on, it's nothing like that," he said softly, his mouth halfway between a smirk and a smile.

Trusting him for reasons she didn't know, Patrice reluctantly followed him into the bedroom.

In stark contrast to the rest of the apartment, the small bedroom was amazingly clean. Against one wall, with Monty's jacket thrown carelessly across the lower bed, was a neatly made bunk bed. Against another wall, under a window, was a poorly painted pink crib, where a one-year-old girl slept peacefully, thumb in mouth.

Against the third wall, crammed next to the closet door, was a desk, currently occupied by a boy who looked seven or eight.

"You're smart, right?" asked Monty, looking straight into Patrice's eyes. "You get good grades and stuff?"

The questions took Patrice by surprise. "Yeah, I guess."

"What do you mean you guess? What kind of grades do you get? What did you get on your last report card?" snapped Monty, seeming annoyed at her spineless answer.

Patrice felt her face get warm, and she muttered, "All A's."

"All A's!" exclaimed Monty, sounding both surprised and impressed. "Dang. I was right about you. You smart, all right. Good. Michael here needs help with his schoolwork. My grades, they pretty much stink. He needs to be helped by someone who does the school thing right."

Michael, who had been quietly watching them talk, looked embarrassed at the mention of his name.

Patrice glanced from Michael to Monty and felt relief flood through her body. Schoolwork was about the only thing she felt comfortable doing, and it was the one thing at which she was very good.

"Sure. Is there a problem he doesn't understand or something?" she asked, smiling at Michael, who seemed even more embarrassed at her question.

Monty looked down at Michael and put his hand on

Patrice's back. He gently guided her out into the hallway, closing the door behind him. The warmth of Monty's hand made her shiver. She took a step away and turned to face him.

"See, Michael is, like, way behind in school. He's been shuffled around a lot, and I think he missed a ton of school. He's been with his—our—daddy for all his life, so there's no telling where he's been or if he even went to preschool or anything like that. He's in first grade, but he don't really know his letters good yet, and he's even worse with numbers and stuff. So I was thinking that you could, like, tutor him after school until he gets caught up. I think he'll listen to someone like you. I mean, you're smart and everything. He needs someone gentle-like to help him. I ain't really got the patience to teach him right. I tried to tell my moms about him, but she . . . Anyway, can you help him?"

Monty looked intently into Patrice's eyes. She didn't know why, but she really wanted him to be pleased with her. "Sure, no problem. I help my cousins a lot. Tomorrow would be good. Do you think he could come up to my auntie's apartment after school so I can help them all at the same time?"

Monty's face seemed to brighten, and Patrice realized that he had thought she would refuse him this small favor. How could she have said no, after all the times he had protected her?

"Yeah, that's cool. We'll be up tomorrow." He gave her a smile, which made her stomach flutter, and they started for the door.

"Great." Patrice paused. She really wanted to thank him for sticking up for her. "Monty?"

Monty opened the front door and slouched casually against the door frame. "Yeah?"

"I—" began Patrice. She looked down at her feet and nervously ran her hand across her hair. "I'll be ready at about four-thirty, so send him up then."

As usual she had chickened out.

"All right. Tomorrow at four-thirty. Cool," Monty said.

"Yeah, okay. Good. See ya."

"Later."

Patrice stepped out into the hallway feeling strangely happy.

Half skipping, half walking, she pranced down the hall to the stairs. With a last glance back she saw that Monty was watching her with a smile—no, maybe it was a smirk—on his face. Embarrassed, she gave him a little wave, then turned and walked with much more dignity to the stairwell.

2

As patrice walked to school the next day, she barely noticed the cold. For her, school was one of the few places she felt good, felt normal. Well, actually, *class* was where she felt normal. In the cafeteria, in gym, in the halls, Patrice felt more like a mouse trying to make it to the cheese before the cats got it. Yeah, that was Patrice: a small, skinny, unwanted mouse, surrounded by well-dressed cool cats with nice hair.

King Middle School wasn't the best school, but it was the only one within walking distance of Auntie Mae's. Patrice had heard that the Ida B. Wells Middle School on the North Side had more accelerated classes, better teachers, and better resources, but she wasn't in that district. Besides, the parents there had to do twenty-five hours of volunteer work. There wasn't any way Auntie Mae could put in that much time, and Patrice would never dream of asking her to. But the teachers at King seemed to really like Patrice. In fact, the only people at King who spoke to her on a regular basis *were* the teachers.

Usually Patrice tried to time her arrival so that she missed the gauntlet in the hall before her first class, but today she was so deep in thought, reliving the night before, that her timing was off. It wasn't until she heard Eddie's familiar nasal tone that she realized it.

"Well, Puffy the Magic Hairdo has arrived," he sneered.

"Shut up, Eddie," snapped Monty. "Hey, Patrice. Back up, y'all. Let her through."

Eddie looked a little taken aback by Monty's quick command. Usually he got more jokes off before Monty said anything. The others looked mildly surprised, but as usual did the bidding of their leader.

Patrice shot a grateful, full-faced smile toward Monty and hurried inside. She was feeling almost happy when she heard Chanterelle Hall and Sarah Tompkins, *the* eighth-grade girls at school. They came up behind her as she was shoving her books into her locker.

"Yo, Puffy," called Chanterelle.

"Hello, Chanterelle," muttered Patrice. Girls like Chanterelle and Sarah always made Patrice feel small, young, underdeveloped, and funny-looking. Dressed in baggy Hilfiger jeans and a Fubu sweatshirt, Chanterelle looked feminine despite her boyish hip-hop clothing. Sarah's style was the opposite: skintight knit pants, black high-heeled boots, and a snug Calvin Klein sweater. In her hand-me-down Levi's and too-big sweatshirt, Patrice felt like a fashion don't.

"Hey, girl, we saw your big sis last night at the hairdresser," said Sarah.

Patrice noticed the new hairstyle she had, an updo that made her look more seventeen than thirteen. Wondering how she slept without messing it up, Patrice pulled out her English folder and slammed her locker shut.

"Yeah, was the shop busy?" she asked, not really caring. She hadn't seen her sister in almost a week, which wasn't unusual.

"Girl," answered Chanterelle, "if you would ever go in and get something done with all that good hair of yours, you would know that the shop is always full. Shoot. All the new customers have to either get up and go in at six a.m. and hope they get done by eight, or go in after work and hope they get home before midnight. It's a good thing we can go there right after school; otherwise we'd never get home. I bet you could get your hair done for free!"

Chanterelle also had a new hairstyle that Patrice

thought made her look too old for anything good to come of it.

Sarah hooted. "That's right. If *my* sister was the best hairdresser in the neighborhood and I had all the hair *you* got, I'd be looking too good, with a new hairdo every other day."

Patrice looked at them and shrugged. There was no use explaining that she hardly knew her sister. What would they say if she told them that Cherise only came home for a fresh change of clothes or to sleep for what seemed like days on end?

Patrice and her sister were extremely different. Cherise was now eighteen, a high school dropout who was lucky enough to be a great hairstylist. Curvy and dressed to kill all the time, she loved a party and always wanted to be surrounded by people. Cherise was worldly and talkative.

This past year was the first time Patrice and her sister had even lived in the same place. Cherise had been raised by their mother in Chicago, while Patrice had been raised by her father's mother in Georgia.

"Yeah, well, class is gonna start," muttered Patrice, anxious to end the conversation. "I'll see y'all later."

Chanterelle and Sarah smirked at each other and parted so Patrice could make her escape. But she'd taken only a step away from the locker and the two fashion plates when she heard her name called again.

"Yo, Patrice!"

Patrice was about to grimace, but stopped mid-frown when she realized that whoever had called her had used her real name. Turning, she came face to face with Monty.

"Hi, Monty," she answered, noticing the slightly shocked looks on Chanterelle's and Sarah's faces. "What's up?"

"Hey, I just—" started Monty.

"Hi, Monty, looking good as always," interrupted Chanterelle, sidling up to Monty and boldly wrapping her arm around his.

"Yo, Chanterelle, you looking good, too," Monty said, turning his attention to the pretty, light-skinned girl.

Patrice felt her heart tighten and she bit her lip in disappointment. But disappointment at exactly what, she didn't know.

"Hey, Monty, you just gonna ignore me?" whined Sarah, stepping in front of Patrice to get closer to Monty.

Patrice watched with both envy and disgust as the two girls flirted effortlessly, and shamelessly, with Monty. After a few moments she'd had her fill and turned to get to class, where she belonged.

"Hey, come back here," Monty called after her.

She sighed, stopped at the door to her class, and waited as he coolly jogged toward her.

"Yes?" she said, feeling suddenly very annoyed at him. "What is it?"

Monty looked down at her intently, not saying a word. He seemed to study her face for a moment, then gave her his half smile, half smirk.

"Hey, I wanted to make sure it's still okay for me to bring Michael up to your place after school today."

"Of course, I said it was okay last night," said Patrice.

Monty seemed surprised, but not angry, at her curt tone. Actually, Patrice was a little surprised at her tone, too. She usually didn't show her emotions, except when she cried. She also didn't really know why she was so annoyed at Monty.

"Yeah, just send him up at about four-thirty," she said in a softer, more normal voice. "The bell's about to ring; you'd better get to class."

Monty leaned against the doorjamb as if he had all the time in the world and looked at her again.

Patrice felt her face get warm under his close scrutiny. She looked down at her feet. "What?" she asked, directing her question to her shoes rather than to the boy in front of her, as she became more and more uncomfortable with his silent staring.

"I think I'll bring him up myself," he finally said. "If that's okay with you."

Patrice looked at him and shrugged. "Yeah, whatever,"

she answered, noticing that he still seemed to be staring at her. "I'll see ya later."

"Yeah, no doubt you will," Monty said as the bell rang.

Patrice felt strangely excited, and relieved, as she finally sank gratefully into her seat.

• • •

The rest of that day was very odd for Patrice. Usually she would go to class, walk through the halls, and have lunch without a single person talking to her. Rasheed or Eddie, or both, would make a snide comment in the hall, but that didn't count. After all, they were talking *about* her, not *to* her. Big difference. But for some reason, this school day found Patrice a much-sought-after girl. Between second and third period, Chanterelle and Sarah had run after her in the hall and practically demanded to know why Monty wanted to talk with her so badly. Patrice instinctively knew that Monty would not want anyone to know his business, especially those two, so she'd enjoyed the pleasure of not telling them anything about what appeared to them to be a really juicy secret. Of course, it wasn't at all juicy, but they thought it was, and it was killing them not to know why Monty had left them so quickly to catch up with Patrice.

Between fourth period and lunch, Raven Brown, another somewhat popular and fashionable girl from the in crowd, had walked with Patrice to the cafeteria, all the while asking her why Chanterelle and Sarah thought she and Monty might be going out. That question made Patrice laugh out loud. Raven even sat down and ate with her, but only because she wanted to be the one to get the scoop. Usually Patrice ate alone reading a book, which she preferred, especially to Raven's company.

Patrice wasn't a big fan of Raven's. She thought Raven's name was eerily accurate. Raven was a big black girl with little eyes and a harsh voice. She always seemed to hover around the edges of a conversation, picking up bits of gossip and spitting out the information to anyone who would listen. Patrice had read someplace that ravens were known for eating dead bodies after battles and were sometimes associated with death and disaster. With her nasty habit of spreading gossip, even if it hurt other people, Raven was just like the bird.

Raven's eyes had almost popped out when Monty sauntered over to their lunch table, leaned between them, and said to Patrice, "We're still on for this afternoon, right?"

Patrice had smiled at him and answered simply, "Of course." Raven's mouth had dropped open.

By the end of the day, the entire school, or at least the entire eighth grade, must have known that something was going on between Monty and Patrice. There hadn't been bigger news than this since a boy named Malik Sellers had gotten arrested in social studies for selling pot out of the last stall of the first-floor boy's restroom.

For Patrice the attention was a new, and rather exhausting, experience. At the final bell she sat in her chair and waited for the halls to clear before leaving the room, hoping that the gossips had started for home. Then, just when she thought she could have a nice, quiet, cold walk home, she heard her name called out for what seemed the millionth time that day. It was the principal, Mrs. Hutton.

"Yes, Mrs. Hutton?" answered Patrice, wondering what she could have done to get the principal's attention.

"I would like a word with you before you leave. Follow me, please."

Mrs. Hutton led Patrice into her office and pointed to a chair. "I have been looking at your transcripts. You have excellent grades."

"Thank you, Mrs. Hutton. I try," answered Patrice.

"So it seems. I received some information regarding a scholarship competition that I think you should enter," said Mrs. Hutton, holding up a thick stack of paper. "There's an African American boarding school called—"

"Dogwood Academy!" shouted Patrice. The feeling of hope she had experienced yesterday came flooding back. She felt her face light up.

Mrs. Hutton smiled and nodded. "That's correct. Dogwood Academy. It's in Mississippi—an excellent institution, one of the few African American boarding schools in the country, and probably the best. The scholarship contest is for students who have shown exceptional academic promise. I would like you to enter the competition. Your test scores are excellent and your writing skills extraordinary, according to your teachers."

"Thank you, ma'am." Patrice was practically shaking with excitement.

"Well, there is quite a lot to do and all applications must arrive at Dogwood by February 21. I think you are quite capable of winning a scholarship, and while I hate to lose such a fine student, it would be a wonderful opportunity for you. Here is the material that you need to get to me no later than February 18. Our school district's applications are to be sent under one cover on the nineteenth. I must stress the importance of getting all the materials completed no later than the eighteenth, so I can deliver them to district headquarters in time. Please let me know if you need any assistance. I've already told your teachers that you would be approaching them for letters of recommendation, and they were more than willing to write them for you."

"Thank you so much, Mrs. Hutton," said Patrice, clutching the packet to her chest.

Mrs. Hutton smiled. "It's my pleasure. Work hard on it and I know you'll win one of the three scholarships."

That day, with thoughts of Mississippi floating through her head, Patrice's walk home didn't seem so cold.

3

PATRICE ARRIVED HOME a little later than usual because of her meeting with Mrs. Hutton. It was after three-thirty, and when she'd settled yet another argument between MarcAnthony and Nefrititi, she found that she barely had time to start dinner and her own homework before there was a knock on the door.

"Hey, Monty. Hi, Michael, how are you today? Ready to do some homework?" asked Patrice, showing them both into the apartment. Patrice called Nefrititi and MarcAnthony to the dining room table and busied herself getting them started on their own homework. Talking to her cousins about their work helped soothe her nerves. She had thought that Monty would just be dropping Michael off, but it appeared that he intended to stay, which made her feel jittery. Monty, on the other hand, seemed as calm as ever.

Patrice watched as he surveyed the place. She had always thought of the apartment as messy, but that was before seeing the one in which Monty lived. Now she decided that the apartment was simply cluttered with knickknacks. Auntie Mae had a penchant for gathering figurines and picture frames. Patrice was in charge of dusting them, naturally.

Monty looked at the dozens of photographs, stopping at an old picture of Auntie Mae and her brothers and sisters.

"That one your moms?" he asked, pointing to an old photo of Patrice's mother.

"Yes," she answered, looking at the picture.

"She's very pretty," he said, picking it up and studying it.

"Yeah, I guess." Patrice shrugged. She hadn't quite forgiven her mother for taking her away from her grandmother and bringing her to Chicago, then going to jail two months later. Thinking about her grandmother always gave Patrice's heart little stabs of pain. To Patrice, it seemed that her leaving had made her grandmother give up on an active life. The cards and letters that Patrice regularly received from her were full of complaints about new aches and pains and life at the nursing home she'd moved to after Patrice left.

"You look just like her," Monty said, pulling Patrice back to reality. He looked at Patrice, studying her face as he had her mother's picture.

Patrice shrugged again. "I guess."

"Do you get all those A's by guessing?" he asked, setting the picture carefully back in its place.

Patrice smiled. "No, I study, which is why you brought Michael here, so we had better get started. Michael, why don't you do this worksheet I found and then you can read to me a little, okay?"

Patrice cleared the table and showed Michael to his seat. Monty wandered over to the table and pulled up a chair next to Patrice.

"Where's your aunt?"

"Let's see. It's Friday, so she had to go to her other job. She usually leaves just a little before I get home. She works Monday, Wednesday, and Friday evenings at that new restaurant on Sixteenth Street. She won't be home till late tonight."

"Well, how 'bout Michael and me just come up the days she works late?"

"I."

Monty looked at her, his eyebrows raised. "What? You what?"

"I. It's Michael and I," corrected Patrice.

"Whatever. You're supposed to be tutoring him, not me."

"Sorry. That schedule works for me."

"Cool. Get started."

"Geez. Yes, sir."

For the next hour Patrice tutored Michael, who, after his initial shyness, opened up to her. Patrice could tell he was a smart kid because he learned quickly. She couldn't help wondering how he could have gotten so far behind. Nefrititi was in the same grade, but she was a much better reader and was getting really good at simple addition and subtraction. From all the time Patrice had spent helping Nefrititi with her homework, she was able to quickly figure out what Michael's weak spots were. He didn't even know the easy words, such as *dog, cat*, and *the*. He also kept mixing up the numbers 2 and 5, and the numbers 6 and 9. As for addition and subtraction, he didn't seem to be familiar with the concepts. Excited about the challenge of helping him catch up, Patrice quickly formulated a study plan in her mind.

She had assumed Monty would go hang out with his friends, but he stayed the entire time, alternately looking at the family pictures in the apartment and sitting opposite Patrice and Michael. Throughout the session, Patrice was acutely aware of his watching and listening. It made her stomach feel funny.

By the end of the hour, Patrice could tell that Michael was fading. He could focus intensely, but he was young and tired pretty quickly. By five-thirty he started squirming in his seat and rubbing his eyes. It became obvious that he needed a break.

"Okay, Michael," said Patrice, patting him on his shoulder. "You did a great job today. We'll work some more next time, 'kay?"

"Okay, thank you, Miss Patrice," said Michael in a quiet, polite way.

"Hey, it's just Patrice, okay?"

"Yes, ma'am."

Patrice smiled at him and was rewarded with a gap-toothed, shy smile.

"Michael, would you like a snack?" she asked, heading toward the kitchen.

Nefrititi, who, to Patrice's delight, had remained silent and courteous throughout the study session, quickly reverted to her true self upon hearing the word *snack*. "I want something, too!" she whined.

"All right, all right, let's see. How about some graham crackers and milk?" suggested Patrice.

"Whatever," said Nefrititi, now boldly staring at Michael, who was doing his best not to look her way. "Hey, I know you," she shouted suddenly, poking Michael in the shoulder to get his full attention. Nefrititi liked having people's full attention. "You go to my school. You always sit alone at lunch, and you're in Mrs. Casson's class, ain't you?"

"*Aren't* you," said Patrice automatically. She handed a plate of crackers to Monty.

"Yes," mumbled Michael, staring at a cracker and carefully dipping it into his glass of milk.

"Why come you don't sit up with the rest of us from the building?"

"*Why come?* For heaven's sake, Nefrititi," scolded Patrice. "Leave him alone. Let him have his snack in peace. Stop pestering him with your bad grammar."

"Stop being such a nag, Patrice. I'm just asking him a few questions."

"Leave him alone for now, okay? Sorry, Michael, she can be a little bold sometimes."

Monty, who had watched this exchange with his smile/smirk on his face, turned to Patrice. "There's nothing wrong with being bold. There's a person I know who ought to be a little bolder sometimes. Finish up, Michael, it's getting late. I need to pick up Mia and the others from Mrs. Robinson's. I'm sure she's handled them too long for today."

"Who's Mia?" asked Nefrititi, turning her attention to Monty.

"She's my little sister," answered Monty, looking amused by the dark little girl who was obviously afraid of nothing.

"Is she my age? Can she play with me?"

"Nah, she's a baby, just turned one."

"Oh."

"Until yesterday, I didn't know you had so many brothers and sisters," said Patrice as she walked Monty and Michael to the door.

"I have four brothers and one sister . . . that I know of," replied Monty curtly.

"Oh. Okay." Patrice quickly changed the subject. "I wish my aunt would have Mrs. Robinson babysit Marc-Anthony and Nefrititi more. It worries me that she sometimes leaves them alone."

"Well, you're around most of the time," said Monty. "I wouldn't stress."

Patrice turned to Michael. "I guess I'll see y'all Monday. Have a good weekend."

"Thanks, Miss Patrice," replied Michael.

"It's just Patrice, Michael, 'kay?"

"Thanks, Patrice," said Monty. "See you around."

"Yeah," answered Patrice. "Sure."

4

SINCE IT WAS THE WEEKEND, Patrice didn't expect to see Monty around at all. This thought didn't surprise her. After all, she had no idea what other kids her age did on Saturdays and Sundays. What *did* surprise her was that she felt disappointed.

Saturday morning, Patrice got up early—even earlier than usual. She wanted to get all her chores done so she could head to the library. She often spent the entire day at the library, but today she was going with a purpose. As long as her chores were finished, Auntie Mae didn't care how long she was out of the apartment. Patrice wanted to complete as much of the application for the Dogwood Academy scholarship as possible. She planned to give it to Mrs. Hutton and ask her to see what needed to be changed or corrected before it had to be turned in. With only five and a half weeks to get everything together, Patrice wasn't going to wait until the last minute.

So, after cleaning the bathroom, doing a couple of loads of laundry, mopping the kitchen floor, and dusting the hundreds of knickknacks and picture frames, Patrice headed for the local library. She got there at 9:10, just minutes after they opened their doors.

The nearest public library was small, old, and underused, but it was a haven for Patrice. An ancient, hardworking, overambitious furnace kept the library a little too warm, and the wooden shelves were filled with a collection of worn and tattered books.

On any given weekend, Patrice could be found nestled into one of the shabby armchairs reading one of the dog-eared books. Today, however, she was working. She found an almost hidden corner with a desk and chair, spread out her materials, and started filling out the application. In addition, she would have to write a two-page personal statement and a three-page essay about either a famous African American or a historical event that was relevant to African American history.

Patrice concentrated on making sure the application was as neat as possible. She was happily writing away when the deep quiet of the library was broken by two familiar voices.

"Man, why are we here?" whined the first voice.

"Man, shut up," said the second. "Like you got someplace better to be."

"Any place is better than this dry ole place," said the first voice. "What we looking for anyway?"

"It's a library, fool," answered the second curtly. "I'm looking for a book."

"Why you need a book?"

"Dang. You know what? You can go home," said the second voice, clearly irritated. "You ain't no help no way."

The voices were very close now. Patrice quietly stood up and peeked around a tall row of books into the next aisle. There she saw Monty scanning the shelves, while Rasheed shuffled impatiently from one foot to the other. Patrice shrugged and was about to go back to work when Rasheed spotted her.

"Yo, it's Puffy the Magic Hairdo!" Rasheed shouted, prompting an annoyed glance and a shush from the lone librarian.

Patrice groaned and tried to shrink behind the desk.

Rasheed rounded the bookshelf, followed by Monty.

"Yo, Puffy, you should be at the beauty shop instead of the library," scoffed Rasheed, clearly happy now.

"Man, shut up," said Monty. "Hey, Patrice, what's up?"

"Hi, Monty."

There was a moment of silence. Rasheed bounced

from foot to foot, looking irritated that he couldn't harass Patrice to entertain himself. Patrice straightened her papers; she wished they would leave so she could get back to work. She didn't mind Monty being there, but Rasheed always gave her the creeps. He scared her a little.

While Eddie was a smart-mouthed bully who never failed to hurt her feelings, Rasheed reminded Patrice of a mean junkyard dog she used to walk by on her way to and from her school in Georgia. The dog was always on a leash, but growled so menacingly at everyone and pulled at his rope so furiously that you knew that if he ever got loose, there'd be no end to the trouble he would cause. As far as Patrice was concerned, Rasheed was the crazed dog and Monty was his leash.

Looking back up at them, she found that Monty, as usual, was watching her intently.

"What are you working on?" he asked, looking at the form with Patrice's neat handwriting on it.

Patrice opened her mouth, glanced at Rasheed, who was sneering at her, and shrugged.

Monty turned to Rasheed. "Man, take off. I'll meet you at Eddie's in a couple of hours, 'round one."

"Whatever. If you want to waste your time here, that's on you. Just be sure to meet me there. Later, man." Rasheed shot a nasty look at Patrice and sauntered down the aisle toward the door.

Patrice let out a sigh of relief at his departure.

Monty turned to Patrice and repeated his question. He walked to the back of Patrice's chair and leaned over her, looking at the papers.

Patrice squirmed, then swiveled around so she could see his face. "It's an application to Dogwood," she answered, wishing he wouldn't lean so close to her. It made her feel hot and uncomfortable.

"What's Dogwood?" he asked, straightening up and leaning casually against the desk.

Patrice sighed. It was obvious she wasn't going to get back to her work, at least not until Monty's curiosity was satisfied. So she sat back, ran a nervous hand across her hair, and launched into a general explanation of the application and Dogwood Academy. Unfortunately, each time she tried to gloss over a detail, Monty would stop and ask questions, until she found it was easier to tell him everything.

"So next year you'll be in Mississippi," stated Monty.

"Only if I get one of the scholarships."

Monty stared at Patrice; as usual, too many looks crossed his face too fast for Patrice to figure out what he was thinking or feeling.

"You'll get one," he said. "And you'll go. Isn't that what you want?"

"I guess," muttered Patrice, her hand again trying to smooth out her hair.

"Jesus!" snapped Monty. "I guess, I guess," he

mimicked. "Patrice, you can't be such a punk all the time."

His words and his sharp tone hurt Patrice. She shrugged and looked down at her paper, trying to keep him from seeing the tears that were forming in her eyes. "Monty, I really need to get back to work," she muttered, careful not to look up at him.

Monty stood there, unmoving. She shot a quick glance at his face. The look on it told her that he hadn't meant to hurt her feelings. Patrice realized that her timidity got on his nerves. But she just couldn't seem to help it. She sat there in silence, not knowing what to say next.

He finally shrugged. "All right," he said. "I was just looking for a book that Michael might be able to read for his book report." He paused. "Patrice, I didn't mean to yell at you. I just wish—" He stopped. "I'll talk with you later." He turned and walked down the aisle, heading back to where he'd been when she first spotted him.

Patrice sighed. She could hear him in the renewed silence of the library pulling out and replacing book after book. She found both his presence, though a few rows away, and the noise he was making to be very distracting.

After a while she got up and walked over to Monty. "These books aren't right for Michael; he's not at this level yet. You should probably look over there." She pointed across the library to the picture-book section.

"Actually, you should have brought him here to choose for himself. But I'll help you pick out something. Where is Michael anyway? Why didn't he come?"

Monty followed Patrice over to the correct section, not bothering to answer any of her questions. "I should have known you'd know where to look. As much time as you spend here," he replied.

"You don't know how much time I spend here."

"That's what you think."

• • •

For the next hour, Monty and Patrice scoured the picture books, looking for one that Michael could read for his report. It seemed to Patrice that finding the right book for the first-grader was taking much longer than necessary. It also appeared to Patrice that whatever book she suggested wasn't right. They were sitting on the floor in front of a growing pile of books, with Patrice making all the suggestions and Monty rejecting each one in turn.

"Okay, how about *Bread and Jam for Frances?*" she said, handing the book over to Monty for inspection.

He looked at the cover.

"Nah, that's a girl book. She's a girl, ain't she?" he said, handing the book back to Patrice.

"It's a badger."

"Yeah, a girl badger."

"Whatever. Okay, how about *The Cat in the Hat?*" Patrice said.

"It looks pretty long," said Monty.

"Monty, we have been through at least twenty books and you've found something wrong with all of them. Why don't you bring Michael here and let him choose?"

"Yeah, I guess that would be cool." Monty stood up and stretched. "You're still going to be here for another hour or so? I mean, you do live here on Saturdays, right?"

"Very funny."

"Are you?"

"You act like you know everything about me."

"I do," said Monty, extending a hand to help her off the floor. "Not everything, but more than you'd think."

"Yeah, whatever, Mr. Know-it-all. Yes, I still have a bunch of work to do on the application," said Patrice, getting to her feet with Monty's help.

"Cool," said Monty. "Don't go anywhere. I'll be back."

Patrice glanced at the clock over the librarian's desk. "Don't you have to meet Rasheed somewhere?"

Monty laughed. "Oh, snap! I forgot all about that boy. Oh well."

"Won't he be upset?" asked Patrice. She remembered how Rasheed had told Monty to show up. She was sure that he'd be annoyed.

"Probably, but so what," answered Monty.

He strolled out of the library, leaving Patrice standing in the middle of it staring after him and wondering how he knew that she spent so much time there on the weekends. She shrugged. Then she returned to the desk and got back to work on the application.

By the time Monty and Michael returned, she had finished all but one section. It was the one that had to be filled out by parents, and she was staring at it, wondering what she was going to do. She was thinking that her only option was to ask her sister, Cherise, to help her get to her mother when Monty and Michael appeared.

"Yo, Patrice."

"Hey, Monty. Hi, Michael, you doing okay?" she said with a smile. Her heart went out to Michael, probably because his shy ways reminded her of herself.

"Hello, Patrice," Michael said softly.

"So, you have to do a book report for school, eh?" said Patrice, standing. "Come on, let's find a good book for you." She offered him her hand, and hand in hand they walked back to the section where she and Monty had spent a fruitless hour.

"Okay, let's see." Patrice grabbed the book nearest her. "Oh, how about *Bread and Jam for Frances?*"

Michael took the book and looked at it closely. "Ain't that a girl?" he asked, pointing to the picture on the cover.

"It's a badger." Patrice sighed.

Monty burst out laughing. Patrice took a swat at him

and missed. Monty laughed louder and then plopped down on the floor next to her.

After fifteen minutes or so, Patrice began to understand why Monty had been so particular. For someone so quiet and polite, Michael wasn't easy to please.

Patrice was running out of ideas when she got a brainstorm. "Oh!" she exclaimed. "I think I've got it." She scrambled to her feet, walked to another bookshelf, brought back a book, and dropped it in Michael's lap.

"*Whistle for Willie?*" read Monty, looking over at the colorful book.

"Yep, I think this is a great book for Michael," replied Patrice. "My cousin MarcAnthony loved it. I'll read it to you, Michael. And, it's about a boy."

Patrice read the book aloud, and when she finished, both Monty and Michael were grinning.

"Patrice, will you teach me to read it all?" asked Michael.

"Of course I will. We'll start Monday."

Patrice stood up and stretched. She looked at the clock. "Geez, it's already three!"

Monty pulled up his sleeve, looked at his watch, and shrugged.

"Whoa. Nice watch, Monty." Patrice was surprised to see him wearing such a fancy, expensive-looking watch. She wondered briefly where he'd gotten it.

"Thanks. You got somewhere to go?" he asked her as he helped Michael put his coat on.

"I need to get dinner started." Patrice figured her work on the application for this weekend was over. Tomorrow she would have church, and by the time she got home and made sure her homework was finished, it would be time to cook dinner. She would have to start writing the essays next weekend. She walked back to her spot. Monty and Michael followed her.

"Start dinner?" asked Monty. "Why you got to cook dinner? Ain't your auntie home?"

Patrice shrugged. "That's just one of my chores. Besides, to be honest, my auntie's a pretty bad cook."

"What else?"

"What else what?"

"What else you got to do at your auntie's? What other chores?"

Patrice neatly arranged her papers and put them into her folder. "Oh, you know: dusting, vacuuming, doing the laundry, cleaning the bathroom, watching Nefrititi and MarcAnthony, helping them with their homework, and cleaning the kitchen. That's all."

"That's all? Sounds like a whole lot to me," blurted Monty. He stood and watched Patrice organize her things and put them into her backpack. "Come on, girl, you're moving slower than molasses."

49

Patrice looked up at him, startled. "Are you waiting for me?"

"Duh. You going home, right?"

"Yes, but . . ."

"Yes, but what?"

"Are you going home, too?"

"Duh. I have to take Michael home."

"Oh. I can get him home if you want me to," offered Patrice.

"Let's go," answered Monty.

Outside it had begun to snow. Big puffy snowflakes, which would be gray slush by tomorrow, were floating softly in the air.

Monty and Patrice walked quietly for the first few blocks, watching Michael run around in the snow, hands in his mittens, arms held high above his head, trying to catch the snowflakes.

"Why you got to do so much at your auntie's?" asked Monty suddenly, breaking the silence.

"I don't know. I just do," said Patrice quietly. She didn't want to tell Monty that she was doing the chores assigned to her sister, as well as her own chores. Since Cherise was never around, Patrice had started doing her chores to make sure their aunt didn't have any reason to kick her out. Also, doing as much as she could at the apartment was the only way Patrice felt she could pay her aunt back for letting her stay there. She strongly suspected that her aunt had taken the second job because of the extra cost involved in caring for her. Patrice knew her aunt loved the fact that Patrice did just about everything around the apartment, and Patrice didn't mind the chores. It wasn't as if she had much else to do anyway.

"Don't you have chores and stuff at home?" she asked, hoping to take the focus off her life.

"Yeah, I guess," answered Monty. He reached over and took the backpack out of Patrice's hand. "I sometimes watch my brothers and sister and stuff when Mom is busy. But it's nothing like what you do. Put your hands in your pockets before they freeze. Them gloves of yours can't be much help."

"Thanks, Monty. Why are you so nice to me all the time?" blurted Patrice.

Monty slowed down and turned to her. As usual, he was looking at her intently—and inscrutably. Replying slowly, as if considering exactly what to say, he answered, "Why shouldn't I be?"

"No one else is," pointed out Patrice, turning at the next street. She knew it sounded a little self-pitying, but she couldn't help it.

"I can't control anyone else," he answered, stopping in his tracks. "Why you going that way? This way is shorter."

Patrice stopped. She always went the long way to avoid the corner store, where Chanterelle, Sarah, and the rest of their group sometimes hung out. It was habit, but she didn't want to admit that to Monty. So instead she opted for a half-truth. "I was enjoying our walk, that's all," she said. Actually, that was a full truth. She couldn't remember when she'd had a more pleasant walk—especially in the middle of winter.

Monty smiled. A real smile this time, with no trace of smirk in it. "Yeah. That's cool. Yo! Michael, this way."

They walked the rest of the way home in silence.

5

SUNDAY PASSED as all Sundays did—rushing to church, cooking after church, then doing homework. Patrice was cleaning the kitchen after dinner when her sister burst through the door. Cherise was a force of nature. Loud, funny, beautiful, and charming, she managed to get and to do whatever she liked. Even when Cherise was selfish or inconsiderate, which unfortunately was very often, or when she was unreliable and irresponsible, also very often, people seemed to forgive her. Patrice frequently found herself annoyed with her sister, especially when doing a chore that was supposed to be Cherise's. She also found that after a few minutes in her sister's presence, her irritation seemed to evaporate into thin air.

"Hey, y'all!" Cherise shouted, striding into the apartment.

MarcAnthony and Nefrititi ran over and gave her a hug. They both worshipped their older, louder, and prettier cousin. Even Auntie Mae got out of her TV chair to give her wayward niece a hug.

"Yo! Sis! What up?" shouted Cherise as Patrice dried her hands and came into the living room.

"Hi, Cherise," Patrice said softly.

"Y'all got any food left? I'm starving," announced Cherise, plopping down at the dining room table.

"Patrice, don't stand there! Make your sister a plate!" said Auntie Mae, heading back to the living room and her TV chair.

A spark of annoyance flashed through Patrice. She had just finished washing all the dishes and putting the leftovers away. She sighed and went into the kitchen to fix a plate for her sister.

"Thanks, little sis, you're the best," Cherise said between mouthfuls, winking at Patrice. "So, you still doing the school thang?"

The school thang, as if it were a hobby or something. Maybe to Cherise school *was* just a hobby. After all, she'd never bothered to finish high school.

"Yeah. How are things at the shop?" Patrice asked politely. She never knew what to say to her sister.

"The shop is cool. We're busy like you wouldn't believe. It's like I live there!"

"Well, you don't seem to live here," replied Patrice shortly.

Cherise hooted. "You got that right, girl. Usually I crash at a friend's place."

"What friend?"

Cherise grinned and winked at Patrice. "Oh, it depends on who's been the nicest to me that day!"

Patrice didn't want to hear any more and decided to change the subject. "Cherise, have you ever heard of Dogwood Academy?"

"Nah, what's that, a new group? What they sing?"

Patrice laughed. "No, it's a boarding school in Mississippi."

"So, what about it?"

"I'm trying to win a scholarship there, for school."

Cherise looked surprised and pushed her now empty plate away.

Knowing there wasn't much chance of Cherise washing it herself, Patrice picked it up and laid it in the sink to wash later.

"So what are you saying? If you get this scholarship, you'll be going to school in Mississippi?"

"Yeah, I hope."

"Yo! Auntie Mae, did you know about this Doggie

thing?" Cherise called into the living room, getting up and leaving her dirty glass on the table.

Patrice groaned inwardly. She hadn't had the chance to mention it to her auntie.

"What? I can't hear you! MarcAnthony, cut the TV down some."

Cherise pulled Patrice into the living room. "This boarding school Patrice is trying to get into."

Auntie Mae sighed and reluctantly turned her attention from her show to her nieces. "I ain't heard nothing about this." She frowned, looking directly at Patrice. Patrice looked down at her feet. "You trying to sneak around and do something, Miss Patrice?"

"No, ma'am. My principal just gave me the application on Friday. And I didn't really see you much on Saturday and then today was real busy and all," muttered Patrice.

"Yeah, uh-huh," Auntie Mae said, never taking her eyes off Patrice. "Well, I'm listening now."

"Well, Dogwood Academy is the best African American boarding school in the country and they are awarding three full scholarships to black kids with good grades and my principal thinks I could win one and she gave me the forms to fill out and I have to write a couple of essays and get all the stuff back to her by the end of next month."

"So is this application and essay junk going to mess up getting your chores done?" Auntie Mae asked.

"No, ma'am," Patrice said hurriedly. "Like yesterday I got all the chores done before I even went to the library."

Auntie Mae shrugged and turned back to the show. "Whatever. As long as you keep up with things here. A scholarship mean I ain't got to pay nothing, right?"

"Yes, ma'am." Patrice sighed with relief.

"Well, it'd probably do you a lot of good getting out of here. You ain't fit for city living," mused Auntie Mae. "Course, I sure would miss having you around. You sure do help out a lot. That sister right there of yours ain't good for nothin' but a smile."

Cherise let out a whoop of laughter and reached down to give her aunt a hug around the neck and a kiss on the forehead. "Auntie Mae, you know you love me!" Cherise giggled, totally unapologetic, as her aunt waved her away with a grin.

"Okay, cool. Good luck with all that. I'm bushed. I've been working like a dog," said Cherise, stretching. "I'm going to go to sleep and not wake up until Tuesday morning!"

"Hey, Cherise?" said Patrice, following her back to the bedroom.

"Yeah?"

"On the application it has a section that has to be filled out by my parents."

"And?"

"Well, I don't really want to send it to Mom. What if it doesn't get back in time?"

"Yeah?"

"Well, I was wondering if maybe you could drive me down to Mount Rose one day so she could fill it out."

"I guess so," said Cherise, with a yawn that showed all of her perfect white teeth. "We'll set it up later, 'kay?"

Patrice smiled; she felt a lot of weight lift from her shoulders. "Okay, thanks." She turned off the lights and was about to close the door when something else popped into her head. "Oh, Cherise?"

"Lord, now what is it?"

"Could you give me a retouch tomorrow?"

"Tomorrow's my day off!" whined Cherise. "I don't want to even see or touch my own head on my day off!"

"Please, Cherise! I haven't gotten my hair done since August."

"August! Dang. I bet them naps is rough up in there. I guess I owe you a favor or two for picking up my slack around here. Fine, when you get home from school tomorrow, 'kay?"

"Thanks, Cherise!"

"Yeah, fine, no prob. Just don't get greedy. Now close the door."

Patrice shut the door softly, put a hand to her head, smoothed her hair, and whispered to herself, "Tomorrow."

• • •

Thankfully, school on Monday was a lot more normal for Patrice than it had been on Friday. From all appearances, Chanterelle, Sarah, and Raven had gotten together over the weekend and come up with a different plan of attack. Finding Patrice unwilling to give out any information, they turned their attention to Monty.

Monty seemed to find the whole thing entertaining. Every time Patrice saw him, he was being flirted with and cajoled by one or more of those girls. Apparently he delighted in talking to Patrice in some sort of code whenever one of them was within earshot, utterly confusing Chanterelle, Sarah, and Raven, amusing himself and annoying Patrice.

Walking the halls with Chanterelle and Sarah before first period, Monty called Patrice over and simply said, "The plan hasn't changed, right?"

"The plan?" Patrice looked at him.

"Yeah, you know, the *Whistle* plan," he said with a smirk as the two fashion plates looked from Monty to Patrice, obviously trying to understand.

"Oh, right," Patrice said, figuring that he was referring to Michael's library book. "Yeah. The plan hasn't changed."

Then, between fourth period and lunch, she passed Monty and Raven at the cafeteria door and he called to her, "Same time, same place, right, Patrice?"

"Yes, Monty," she replied, even more annoyed now at the little game he was playing. The last thing she wanted was attention, especially from those three wannabe rap music video babes. The thought that kept her sane was that she was finally going to get her hair done that afternoon.

Ducking out of a side door after school to avoid not only Eddie and Rasheed but also Raven, Sarah, and Chanterelle, Patrice walked quickly home, wanting to get dinner started and her homework done before Monty and Michael got there. She also wanted to talk with Cherise. She couldn't exactly get her retouch done in the middle of the tutoring session. But when she got home, Cherise wasn't there. The only sign of her was a dozen opened soda cans in the living room, a sink full of dirty dishes, and two empty pizza boxes on the kitchen table.

MarcAnthony and Nefrititi were sitting amid the mess watching the one TV show they both liked.

"Where's Cherise?" Patrice asked them.

"She just left," answered MarcAnthony. "She had a whole bunch of friends over and they decided to go to a movie. She let us have the last two sodas, though, and we split the last piece of pizza," he said, gesturing absent-mindedly at a dirty plate and two empty cans in front of them.

"She left a mess," Patrice said, more to herself than to the two kids.

"Yeah, Mama gonna be mad," replied Nefrititi, picking up an empty can and trying to drain the very last drops.

Patrice sighed. Her eyes filled with tears. She didn't know whether she was crying because she would have to clean up or because she knew her sister wouldn't be back to do her hair. She had really been looking forward to getting her hair done.

Swiping at a hot tear that was coursing down her cheek, she snatched the nearest can, grabbed the remote, and punched the off button.

"Y'all get up and help with this mess. I bet you ain't even started your homework," snapped Patrice.

The two spun around and were about to protest, but something in Patrice's face stopped them. Plus, she only used *ain't* when she was mad; it was all that hinted that she had spent her early years in Georgia.

"Patrice, chill, awright," muttered MarcAnthony. "We'll help. But Cherise said we could watch TV."

"Yeah, well, as usual Cherise ain't here, is she? And since y'all drank the soda and ate the pizza, y'all had better help," replied Patrice angrily.

Leaving MarcAnthony and Nefrititi to clean the living room, Patrice stormed into the kitchen, trying to decide whether to start dinner and then clean up the mess, or clean up the mess and then start dinner. She decided to clean first, then start the hot dogs and macaroni and cheese.

She had just finished slamming down the last clean pot when there was a knock on the door. "Now what?" she muttered crankily. She poked her head out of the kitchen and saw MarcAnthony let in Monty and Michael.

"Phooey, I totally forgot about them," she said to herself. "I haven't even gotten to my own homework yet."

"Hey, Patrice," Michael called, smiling his shy smile.

"Hi there, Michael," she answered halfheartedly. She felt frustrated and put-upon.

She quickly got MarcAnthony and Nefrititi started on their homework, and told Michael that they would work on his numbers first, before reading *Whistle for Willie*. While Michael was practicing writing his numbers from 1 to 50, she grabbed her math book and began doing her homework.

Monty, having nothing to do, looked again at the dozens of family pictures. Then, having done that two or three times, he took a seat at the table and rocked back and forth, watching the others, especially Patrice, work.

Patrice was finding it very hard to concentrate with his rocking and his looking, and finally, when he began to drum on the table with his fingers, she slammed her pencil down and glared at him.

"Don't you have homework, or something you could do? Or someplace you could go?" she barked.

Monty stopped his constant motion and stared at Patrice, evidently surprised by her uncharacteristic outburst. His smirk appeared, this time with a raised eyebrow. "What?" he asked, righting his chair and staring at her.

"I said, don't you have homework or something to do that is less disruptive to the rest of us?" Her tone had softened somewhat, but there was still annoyance in her voice.

"Oh," Monty said. "It's like that, huh?" He stood up and sauntered to the door as the others watched him. "Cool." With that, he was gone.

The three young kids looked at Patrice, who sat staring at the door. Her anger ebbed away, but was quickly replaced by another just as unpleasant feeling—regret.

"Come on, guys, finish your work," she said softly, the anger completely gone now. She glanced at Michael's paper. "Good job, Michael. Keep going."

Michael beamed at the praise. He returned to his numbers, his tongue poking out of his mouth as he concentrated.

Patrice tried to finish her own work, but found she couldn't focus on algebraic expressions. It had been easier to concentrate with Monty's noise than with his absence. She felt bad that she had blown up at Monty. He wasn't the one she was upset with. It was her sister who had made her so mad. Not only had she left a mess for someone else to clean up, but she hadn't kept her promise. It didn't surprise Patrice. During one of their few real conversations, Patrice remembered Cherise telling her that life was all about looking out for number one. And in Cherise's world, Cherise was number one.

Patrice smoothed her hair, knowing that the semi-neat ponytail she had pulled it into this morning was probably a distant memory now. Sighing, she decided that she would have to apologize to Monty as soon as possible—if he would speak to her again.

Just then, there was a knock at the door. Nefrititi ran to open it, and Monty strolled in with his backpack in his hands. Not saying a word, he coolly pulled out a math book, a piece of paper, and a pencil, and started doing math.

Michael, MarcAnthony, and Nefrititi shrugged and returned to their homework. Patrice stared at Monty, who, in meticulously neat handwriting, quickly did three math problems flawlessly.

"Monty, I—" began Patrice, stammering.

"Shhhh," Monty said, putting a finger to his mouth. "You're making too much noise and disturbing the rest of us. Please, no talking, it's disruptive."

Patrice's mouth remained open.

Monty chuckled, gave her a wink, and went back to work.

Patrice felt that she still owed him an apology, but Monty seemed totally focused on his work and appeared to be fine. That thought made Patrice happy. Watching him and feeling suddenly at peace, Patrice finally bent to her own work.

6

THE REST OF THE WEEK went by quickly, or so it seemed to Patrice. With only Tuesday and Thursday free, Patrice was suddenly busier than ever. That Wednesday, Monty and Michael had come, right on time as usual, and both had brought their homework. Surprisingly, the same thing happened on Friday. Patrice was stunned to see that Monty had brought homework. After all, it was the start of the weekend. Even she didn't do much on Fridays.

"Your math teacher gave you homework on a Friday?" asked Patrice. She usually just did some reading. She had given Michael a little work to do and he had sailed through it. Now he, MarcAnthony, and Nefrititi were in the middle of a game of Uno.

Monty grinned as he looked up from his math book. "I might be a little behind in my homework."

Patrice smiled back. "Okay, how behind?"

Monty let out a loud gaffaw. "About three months."

Patrice gasped. The thought of being that far behind made her queasy. "No way."

Monty grinned again and shrugged. "This stuff is easy. I'll be caught up in no time."

After watching the way Monty whipped through the problems, each one nice and neat and correct, she didn't doubt it.

"Michael is as smart as you are," she observed more to herself than to Monty. She wondered why Monty wasn't in the accelerated classes with her.

Monty stopped his work and looked up. As usual, Patrice squirmed and looked away. Her stomach felt funny.

"I ain't smart," Monty replied at last. He sounded almost angry.

Patrice frowned slightly. Based on how quickly he could do the math, it seemed to Patrice that he was very smart; he just didn't really care about school.

"Yes, you are," Patrice said firmly, looking directly back at him. "You don't bother to do your work, that's all. It's like you don't care about it."

Monty returned her gaze. He appeared to be thinking about her comment. Then he shrugged. "Yeah, well, I ain't as smart as you are," he finally answered.

This time it was Patrice who grinned. "Yes, well, all of us can't be geniuses."

Monty laughed. "Oh, you think you all that, huh?"

Patrice laughed at the very thought. "Hardly," she said between giggles. "I'm not even half of that!"

She looked at Monty, expecting him to laugh with her, but he was gazing at her in the same old way. She stopped giggling.

He smiled at her, shook his head, and said, "No, Patrice, you *are* all that."

Startled by the compliment, Patrice murmured a soft "Thanks" and retreated into the kitchen. Monty got up and moved his work to the kitchen table, while the kids started yet another game of Uno in the living room, and Patrice began dinner.

She was standing at the stove trying to figure out whether to invite Monty and Michael to dinner or to make extra and *then* invite them to dinner, using the excuse of extra food, when the door flew open and in swooped Cherise.

Right away she noticed Monty. "Well, who might this handsome young man be?" she asked Patrice, her voice full of mirth and her eyebrows raised.

Monty got up from the table and offered his hand. "Monty Freeman. You must be Patrice's sister. Y'all resemble."

Patrice felt a surge of anger at her sister. She was still upset about Monday. She had tried to call Cherise at work on Tuesday, but each time Cherise had been busy with a client, which had annoyed Patrice so much that she had decided to just live with her poof of hair forever rather than hunt down her sister and beg for an hour or so of her precious time. Patrice was just as mad at herself for counting on Cherise. She should have known better.

"You hear that, 'Trice?" hooted Cherise, coming up to Patrice and giving her a big hug, not noticing that Patrice didn't bother to hug her back. "Your boyfriend think we look alike."

Boyfriend? Oh geez. Patrice felt her face get hot. *Why can't Cherise shut up?*

"Cherise, Monty's not—" began Patrice.

But Monty interrupted her. "You work at the Cut'n'Style, right?" he asked.

"Shoot. I work like a dog at the Cut'n'Style, but I ain't never seen you up there. What you know about that place?" said Cherise, making herself comfortable at the kitchen table after fixing a tall glass of ice tea.

"That's where my moms get her hair done," he answered.

Patrice sighed and returned to the cooking.

"Who your mama?" asked Cherise, taking off her high-heeled shoes and moaning with relief.

"Deborah Clark," Monty replied in a voice that caused Patrice to turn and look at him.

"Oh," said Cherise. "Really."

Monty simply nodded.

"What you cooking?" Cherise asked Patrice, obviously changing the subject. She poured herself a second glass of ice tea and then set one down in front of Monty. "Patrice, is your boyfriend staying for dinner?"

Again, Patrice's face got hot. "No, he's not—"

"You can't stay for dinner?" Cherise interrupted, turning to Monty.

"Sure I can," replied Monty.

Patrice saw the familiar smirk creep across his face.

"See, Patrice, he can stay for dinner," said Cherise, smiling down at Monty. "He just said so!"

"No, I meant he's not my—" started Patrice.

This time Monty interrupted her. "Cherise, have you met my little brother? He'll love you."

"Hey, I like me some younger men, and seeing as my sister already got you all snatched up, let's meet the little man. Bet he look as good as you." Cherise laughed, flirtatiously grabbing hold of Monty's arm and making him escort her out of the kitchen.

Patrice heard them in the living room, demanding that they be included in the latest Uno game.

She shook her head. "He's not my boyfriend," she

muttered, but only the hamburger patties were around to hear her.

• • •

Patrice never bothered to ask Cherise about her hair that night. It was too hectic. She finished making dinner, everyone ate, and then they all played a couple more games of Uno. Cherise excused herself, got into the shower, came out looking even more beautiful than usual, and left carrying a huge overnight bag. Patrice figured she wouldn't see her again until the end of next week.

Monty and Michael left shortly afterward. Patrice figured it was because the life of the party, Cherise, had gone.

Patrice cleaned up the kitchen and got MarcAnthony and Nefrititi bathed and in bed. She had planned to curl up under her covers and read some, but the next thing she knew it was Saturday morning.

It was much later than she'd wanted to get up, so by the time she finished her chores and got to the library, it was already past noon. She walked through the book racks to her hidden desk and was surprised to see Monty sitting there, his homework spread out. "Hey!" she said, speaking much too loudly.

"Hey, yourself," he answered, leaning back in the chair. "You're late."

"Late? Late for what?" She set down her book bag and rubbed her hands together, trying to warm them.

"I thought you got here when it opened," he replied, taking her cold hands into his warm ones and rubbing them.

She was so distracted by his gesture, she didn't answer him. She could only stare at their hands, feeling the warmth return to hers.

"You still working on that application?" he asked, dropping her hands and gathering up his books and papers.

"Uh," she muttered, still distracted.

"Is that a yes or a no?" he asked, definitely smirking at her now.

"Oh, yeah, I got two essays I still have to do," she answered, watching him pick up all of his things. "You don't have to move, there's another desk a few rows over by the window. I can work there."

Monty shook his head and pointed to a large empty table that sat in the middle of the room. "Why don't we move there?" he asked.

"We?"

"Yeah, you and me. We."

"I—"

"You what? You want to be alone or something?" Monty asked.

Patrice thought she heard disappointment in his

voice. "It's *you and I*. Why don't *you and I* move over there," she said.

Monty shook his head. "You are something else, Patrice." He laughed. "Shoot, if I keep hanging out with you, I'll be speaking all proper and stuff and I'll lose my ghetto membership card. Come on." He grabbed her book bag and led her to the table.

As he settled down, carefully arranging his stuff, Patrice pulled out her application. She went over everything, then stopped at the parental section and made a mental note to bottle her pride and beg Cherise to drive her to Mount Rose the day after tomorrow. It was Martin Luther King Day, and she was out of school.

Now, which essay should she do first? Deciding on the historical one, she gazed out the window and tried to think of an appropriate figure or event to cover. Suddenly she noticed that Monty had stopped working and was watching her as she chewed her bottom lip.

"You all right?" he finally asked.

"Huh?" she mumbled, pulling herself out of her reverie. "Yeah. Yeah, I'm okay. Just thinking."

"What you thinking about?"

"Oh, what to write this essay on," she said, shoving the instructions over for him to read.

He looked at them. "What about King?"

"Nah, too expected," she said.

"Malcolm X?"

"Nah, too radical. I was thinking of maybe a woman, or someone who was an educator."

"A woman?" Monty sounded incredulous. "Like who? Harriet Tubman?"

Patrice giggled. "Why do you sound so stunned? I was thinking about Mary McLeod Bethune or someone like that."

"Mary McWhat Bewho?" said Monty, leaning back in his chair, looking like his casual self.

"Mary McLeod Bethune, she founded Bethune-Cookman College. She was one of, like, seventeen children of former slaves, and she advised presidents on child welfare and education and stuff like that."

Monty looked interested and that was enough for Patrice. She went to the history section of the library and came back with an armful of books. After showing Monty a few of them, she could tell she had his tacit approval. Feeling buoyed, she went to work.

For the rest of the afternoon, they worked in companionable silence. Patrice finished two drafts of her essay and felt that all she needed was a little time in the school's computer room to polish and print it. And, true to his word, Monty caught up on his math homework.

Even though she had spent it working, this had been one of Patrice's best days since moving to Chicago. Monty looked pleased, too.

It was dusk when they walked home. Opening the

door to the apartment, Patrice found that Auntie Mae had had enough energy to cook and had started making dinner. On the way to her bedroom, she glanced into the bathroom and saw a huge container of relaxer creme next to an even bigger bottle of conditioner.

"Patrice, Cherise said to be home tomorrow after church, 'cause that's when she gonna do your retouch," said Nefrititi, skipping past. "She said she also gonna do something to my head!"

"Yes!" whispered Patrice, running her hand across her puffy ponytail.

Yes, indeed, this had been a very good day.

7

Patrice sat patiently in the kitchen chair while Cherise expertly parted her hair and applied the relaxer creme.

"Lord, girl, you should have asked me about three months ago to do this. You got three, maybe four inches new growth here. Your hair grows too fast to be waiting five months for a retouch. You need one at least every eight weeks, even in the winter," lectured Cherise.

"Yes, ma'am," muttered Patrice. She didn't bother to remind Cherise that she had asked her for a retouch around Halloween. Apparently Cherise had forgotten all about that.

"So, how long you been going out with Monty?" asked Cherise.

"We're not going out," explained Patrice, happy to be able to clear things up so that Cherise wouldn't embarrass her anymore. "I'm helping his little brother get caught up in school, and Monty just brings him here. That's all. He's not my boyfriend."

"Girl, the boy is too cute. You need to grab him if he's available," said Cherise. "If I was four, five years younger, he'd be all about me. Guarantee. You meet his mom yet?"

"No, I've only been to his apartment once, and no one was there except the kids," replied Patrice.

"Yeah, I bet she wasn't there," said Cherise disgustedly. "How many kids she got now, ten?"

"I don't really know. There were only six there: Monty, Michael, three other boys, and a little girl, Mia," answered Patrice. "Why? Do you know his mom?"

"Yeah, her trifling butt is always up in the salon getting some ghetto hairstyle from Termaine, the hairstyling queen of tackiness," said Cherise. "I don't think any of them kids got the same daddy. Plus, Miss Deborah is forever in the club or pregnant. She be bringing all these different men up in the shop, getting them to pay for her hair or nails. Old men, too. Ugh. Then she got the nerve to come in the shop every now and then asking us stylists to lend her money for food. Hell, she always got money when she want to get a new weave or them tacky finger waves. She's too pitiful."

Patrice was silent. She had never really thought about

what Monty's life was like at home. He always seemed too capable and self-assured to have any problems; she had assumed that everything was good for him. Nobody at school had a lot of money, but she had never thought that sometimes Monty didn't have any food in the house. She made a mental note to always invite him and Michael to dinner on tutoring nights.

"Anyway, if he ain't your boyfriend, he sure didn't correct me when I said he was," continued Cherise. "He just grinned."

"Yeah, well, Monty thinks everything is funny," said Patrice. "He probably thought that was the funniest thing he'd heard all day. If he wanted a girlfriend, he'd be going out with Chanterelle or Sarah."

Cherise whooped. "Them ole grown-acting girls? Them girls be knocked up before high school, mark my words. Maybe he want someone quiet and classy like you. Them two young hot mamas ain't about nothing. They can't compete with someone like you."

Patrice smiled at the unexpected compliment. "Thanks for saying so, Cherise. I doubt he would agree, though."

Cherise smiled back at her. "Please, girl. You look too much like me for him to think anything else. Shoot, besides me, you're the classiest girl I know."

Patrice laughed until she saw that Cherise was serious. "Classy" wasn't an adjective she'd use to describe her sister, so she chose not to say a thing.

They were quiet for a while, then Cherise asked, "You hear from Marquis?"

Patrice was surprised by the question. She knew her older brother even less than she knew Cherise. He had been put in juvenile boot camp about a month after she got to Chicago. She probably wouldn't recognize him if he came up to her on the street.

"No," she said. "Why would he be calling me?"

"Yeah, I guess he wouldn't be calling you. You can't help him none," answered Cherise. "That fool call me collect on my cell phone asking for money. Like I got money to give him. Wasting my minutes. You know how much it cost to talk to somebody calling collect from jail? Hey, how your scalp feel? I wanna keep this stuff on for about another three minutes."

"I'm fine for now," replied Patrice. "Why would Marquis need money?"

"Girl, he told me he wanted nine hundred dollars 'cause some lawyer said he could get a shorter sentence for him. I told his dumb butt if he wanted a shorter sentence, he shouldn't have been trying to rob that store with no BB gun. A BB gun! He too stupid. His goofy tail could have gotten killed. Them store owners got real guns. Anyway, I told him I ain't got no money to waste on someone who was guilty nohow. Hell, to be honest, I ain't got no money saved up at all no more. Shoot, I had to spend money at the dentist last month when I had my caps put on. Before that, my raggedy car had the nerve to break down and I had to get it fixed. That cost me three hundred dollars. Then what money I had left I spent on getting my teeth whitened. Now I'm flat busted again. Be a month before I can move out into my own place now."

"You want to move out? But you're never here anyway," remarked Patrice.

Cherise laughed. "Yeah, but I get tired of sleeping here, sleeping there. And if you spend more than one night at some man's house, he think you're all into him. I want my own place, maybe with a roommate. Besides, Aunt Mae don't need another mouth in this apartment.

"That's why it's good that you gonna get this scholarship thing. Of course, then Aunt Mae will have to get her lazy tail up and clean and cook again, but at least it'll only be for her own kids, not Mama's. Then maybe she can quit that second job and get some rest. Tell me more about this Doggie thing."

Patrice giggled. "It's Dogwood Academy. It's one of the few African American boarding schools in the country, and it's the oldest and most prestigious. The brochure says 98 percent of their graduates go to college. That 85 percent of the kids who go there get full-ride scholarships to college. Thirty-six percent of their graduates go to Ivy League schools. It's in Mississippi on this big sixty-acre campus."

"Well, you'll get in. You the smartest person I know."

"Thank you, Cherise. I sure hope I do."

Patrice was silent as Cherise rinsed her hair. She steeled herself to ask her big question.

"Um, Cherise? Do you think you could drive me to Mount Rose tomorrow? I gotta have Mama fill out part of the application. Remember?"

"Yeah. Well, sure, I guess, but it gotta be early. Be ready to go by like eight 'cause I don't wanna waste my whole day with Mama."

"Thanks, Cherise. That would be a really big help."

"Yeah. Now, how you want your hair?"

"Oh, a ponytail is fine."

"Shoot, I didn't spend the last hour retouching and conditioning all this hair for you to pull it back in no funky ponytail."

With that, Cherise worked her hairstyling magic, and when Patrice looked into the mirror it was like seeing someone she didn't know. Gone was the big poof. In its place was a head of shiny black hair that lay calmly and obediently in waves to her shoulders. Cherise had parted it on one side, with diagonal bangs. Patrice thought it looked—well, that *she* looked—pretty.

"Man, thanks, Cherise!" Patrice couldn't believe it and could hardly wait until Monty saw it. She wondered when she had started to care what Monty thought about her. That was something she needed to think about a little more.

Then, as if reading her mind, Cherise laughed and said, "Now, if that Monty don't notice you rocking this fab hairstyle, he ain't got no good sense, or good taste." She looked proudly at her handiwork. "Not that he seemed to mind your hair the way it was. He was all about you. Trust that."

Patrice opened her mouth to protest, but after a quick glance in the mirror, she smiled instead.

• • •

The next morning, Patrice woke up to her alarm clock, which she had set for six. She glanced at Nefrititi's bed, hoping the noise hadn't disturbed her sleep. True to form, Nefrititi was out like a light. That girl was either totally awake or completely asleep. She was beginning to remind Patrice more and more of Cherise.

Patrice bent over to see if Cherise had slept in the bottom bunk bed last night. And, true to *her* form, she had slept elsewhere. Trying to ignore the knot that was gathering in the pit of her stomach, Patrice quietly took her things from the bedroom and went to the bathroom to prepare herself for the day's trip. She smiled each time she looked in the mirror and caught a glimpse of her new hairdo.

By seven she was eating breakfast, and by seven-thirty she had her backpack by the door, ready to go whenever her sister showed up. Eight came and went with no sign of Cherise. As the clock ticked, the knot in Patrice's stomach grew.

At eight-fifteen, she called Cherise's cell phone and left a message. She passed the time by making Auntie Mae breakfast before she left for work at the restaurant, where she was trying to pick up a few extra dollars by working at her second job on a paid day off from her first job. At eight-thirty, Patrice tried Cherise's cell phone again. It rang and rang before going to voice mail.

By nine, both MarcAnthony and Nefrititi were awake, and Patrice made *them* breakfast. The feeling of doom was now overwhelming, and the smell of their breakfast nauseated her. She made a third call to Cherise at nine-thirty and left another message.

At ten-thirty, she called Mrs. Robinson, the building's surrogate grandmother, whom she had asked to watch MarcAnthony and Nefrititi while she was at Mount Rose. She told Mrs. Robinson that she was sorry she hadn't called sooner and it seemed that she wasn't going to need help, after all. At eleven-thirty, when she called Cherise once more, she hung up rather than listen to her recorded music and message again.

Finally, at twelve-thirty, she got a call from Cherise.

"Girl, I forgot all about driving you down to Mount Rose. I left my phone in the car all night, I was so tired! I went to this new club way on the North Side and went to breakfast with some of my girls. It was too wild. We're on our way to the movies, and after that I've gotta get some z's. Sorry about the whole visit-Mom thing. Hope you ain't mad! I'll catch ya later!" Click.

Patrice sighed. Actually, she wasn't even mad, just sad and disappointed.

Pulling out the application, she spread it across the tiny kitchen table and decided to double-check it again. She'd completed everything except her personal statement essay and the parental consent part. At least she could get her second essay finished today.

With the noise of the television and MarcAnthony and Nefrititi's arguing in the background, Patrice went to work on the essay. She found that writing actually made her feel a little better. She was so engrossed in her thoughts, and the words she was using to express them, that she didn't know anyone had knocked on the door until she heard Nefrititi shout, "Hey! We ain't got no homework today. What you doing here?"

Patrice looked up and saw Michael grin at Nefrititi as he followed her into the living room.

Monty strolled into the kitchen. "Hey, girl, what you doing? Whoa, look at you! Check out that hair! Girl, you look smokin'!"

"Hi. Thanks! Cherise did it last night. Monty, what are you doing here?" responded Patrice, yawning as she stood, stretched, and started to shake out her hand. She had been writing so much, and so long, it was beginning to cramp. Monty grabbed it and began rubbing it. Patrice stared as he massaged the aches out of her writing hand. "What's going on?" she managed to ask.

"Nothing. Michael wanted to come up and see if MarcAnthony and Nefrititi could play. Well, actually, if Nefrititi could play. I think he got a crush on her," Monty said with a laugh.

Patrice's eyes were still glued to their entwined hands. Gently, and reluctantly, extracting her hand, she sat back down at the table. Monty sat across from her.

"You're not hanging with your boys today?" she asked, straightening up her papers.

"Nah, them knuckleheads ain't doing nothing," he answered, looking at the papers covered with her handwriting. "At least, they ain't doing nothing good. You doing homework on a day off?" he asked, looking at the papers.

"No, it's the last essay for the Dogwood application," she answered.

"You done with it all now?"

"Yes. No. Almost."

"Which is it? Yes or no?"

"Well, I'm done writing my essays, but I gotta type them both tomorrow after school. And I'm done with the application. But I gotta have my mom fill out a part of it."

"I thought your moms was in jail."

Patrice looked down at the pile of papers. "She is. My sister was going to take me to visit her today," she answered quietly.

"Hey, don't be all embarrassed. My daddy's in jail, the last I heard."

Patrice looked up at him. He didn't seem at all ashamed of his father, but then she remembered the look on his face when Cherise had mentioned his mother. She knew now that the look had been embarrassment. Patrice gave him a weak smile. "Hey, do you guys wanna stay for dinner?"

"You cooking?"

"Of course, who else?"

"What y'all having?"

"Frozen lasagna."

"Sure. Thanks."

"So Mrs. Robinson always watches your other brothers and your sister?"

"Why do you ask?" Monty sounded perturbed.

Patrice turned and looked at him as she got up from the table. He was frowning slightly. She shrugged and smiled at him.

"I don't know. Your little sister was so cute. I was just wondering why you never bring her with you. I mean, you spend a lot of time with Michael, but I never see you with your other brothers or your sister. I was just curious, that's all."

"Oh." He sounded less uptight. "Mia stays mostly with her grandmother. She lives on the fifth floor."

"I didn't know your grandmother lived in this building."

"She don't. *Mia's* grandmother do."

"Oh."

"We ain't got the same daddy. Only me and Michael got the same daddy."

"I see."

"I guess that's why I spend so much time with him. Even though I've only seen my pops like three times. Once, when I was little, he came by with some nasty candy for me—them nasty chocolate coconut things. I hate coconut. That must have been about seven years ago, but the next thing I knew, Mom was pregnant with Michael. Then a few months after Michael was born, he came and got him, saying he was going to raise him. I guess he forgot that *I* was his son, too. Anyway, this past August he came back, bringing Michael and saying he was in a bit of trouble and couldn't take care of him no more. August 11, it was. It was my birthday. He gave me this watch before he left. I didn't even know he knew when my birthday was. I guess seven years between gifts ain't too bad," he finished with a derisive snort.

"It's a very nice watch."

"Yeah. He said it was real expensive, but I didn't believe him until I saw a picture of this same watch in one of the fancy magazines at the doctor's office. Same brand and everything. It cost hundreds of dollars. I knew then it was stolen. That's why he in jail now. For taking stuff people stole and selling it. Fencing is what they call it. Why's your moms in jail?"

Patrice slid the frozen dinner into the oven. Then she sat back down at the kitchen table facing Monty. "Stealing people's information," she said.

"What you mean?"

"Identity fraud. She used to work at this check-cashing place and she would get social security numbers and bank account numbers from the people who came in and give them to her boyfriend. I guess they would use that information for fake IDs and stuff. She had all these different checkbooks for accounts that weren't hers, and all these credit cards with other people's names on them. She was lucky. The judge said that the maximum sentence for identity fraud is, like, twenty-five years. She only got ten years."

Patrice paused. "She got in trouble for welfare fraud, too. She could have gotten another maximum sentence of fifteen years for that. But she was lucky and only got five. Plus the judge said she could serve the two sentences together. So she may be able to get out in, like, eight years with good behavior. Of course, I'll be, like, twenty-one or so by then, so that doesn't really do me any good.

"Anyway, she was also telling Medicaid she had five

kids and was getting way more money than she was supposed to, since she only had Cherise and Marquis. That's
why she came and got me from my grandma's. She said
they mistook the number 3 for a 5 on the application.
She lied. When she came and got me, she said she missed
me and wanted to be my mom and stuff. But all that was
a lie, too. She was just trying to stay out of jail."

"Where is your grandma now?"

"She's in a nursing home, in Georgia."

"What was Georgia like?"

Patrice smiled and looked out of the little window in
the kitchen at the cold gray sky.

"Green and warm." Then, remembering the endless
parade of homemade baked goods, she added softly,
"And sweet."

Monty and Michael left shortly after dinner, giving
Patrice plenty of time to think. Actually, she and Monty
weren't all that different. Both of them had useless moms
and absent dads. Also, even if he wasn't into school the
way she was, he was definitely just as smart. She wondered whether she would be so into grades and stuff if
she was as popular as Monty.

All that night she thought about Monty. She even fell
asleep thinking about him.

8

THE NEXT MORNING, Patrice arranged for time in the computer room. Also, she gave the rest of the application to the principal. She didn't really want to rely on Cherise to get her to her mom, so she swallowed her pride and asked Mrs. Hutton whether, since she lived with her, Auntie Mae could sign the application in place of her mother. Mrs. Hutton said she would look into it. She said it was obvious that Patrice had worked hard on the application and she was very impressed. The recommendations from the teachers were already in, so all she needed were the essays and the parental permission.

Patrice let Monty know that she was staying late at school to type her essays. Watching him walk home with his gang gave her an uncertain feeling. She really didn't know how to describe their relationship. They seemed to be friends, but as long as he hung out with people like Rasheed and Eddie, she would never feel totally comfortable. Now that she knew him better, she wondered more and more why he even bothered with them.

It was almost dusk when she finished her essays and walked home. Monty's gang had long since vacated the stairs in front of the door. That was a good thing, because Monty wasn't there to protect her, as he had been every day for the past couple of weeks. In all that time, neither Eddie nor Rasheed had said more than two words to her. Well, at least not when Monty was with her.

Seeing that the elevator was out again, Patrice started the long climb to the fifteenth floor. When she was just past the ninth floor, she heard the door above her open. Two voices she immediately recognized shattered the cool silence of the stairwell.

"Shoot, man," Rasheed said. "When I'm rich I ain't never gonna live nowhere that got an elevator."

"How you think you gonna get rich?" asked Eddie, laughing.

"Man, by playing ball," answered Rasheed.

"Ball!" snorted Eddie. "Man, you ain't no good. I can whup you with one hand most times."

Patrice shuddered. She was stuck. She was as close to the door on the ninth floor as she was to the door on the tenth. In a second they would see her. There was no escape, really. She knew that they would harass her if they saw her run back down, and they'd harass her if she climbed past them. With a sigh, Patrice tried to steel herself for their nasty comments.

"Check it out, Eddie," sneered Rasheed. "It's Little Miss Hair Weave. How much you pay the horse for the fake hair you got glued to your head?"

Patrice glared and tried to climb past him and Eddie. Eddie stood his ground, blocking her way. Rasheed laughed and brushed rudely past her to the step directly behind her. She was now trapped between them.

"Man, you think this a hair weave? I don't know. Look pretty real to me," said Eddie, putting his hand through her hair. "Let me see."

Patrice whipped her head back and tried to take a step away from him, but managed only to fall off the step and into Rasheed. Rasheed caught her, holding her up with his hands on her waist.

"Shoot, man," Rasheed said, pushing her off him and back onto the step in between them but keeping his hands on her waist. "Maybe Puffy got more to give than we know about. I mean, why else you think Monty be all in her face suddenly?" Rasheed squeezed her waist and slid his hands down onto her hips. "Maybe she ripe."

Eddie hooted with laughter. "You know, my brother, maybe you're right. Maybe *that's* why Monty is sniffing

around her so much. Maybe she is ripe for the picking."
Again, Eddie put his hand in her hair. "Wasn't he saying
the other day that he be getting some of this?"

Patrice couldn't believe what was happening. This
was far worse than their talking about her hair or her
mom.

"Stop it! Let go!"

"Come on, you know you like it, Puffy," replied Eddie,
taking even more of her hair into his hands.

Attempting to twist away from them, Patrice backed
up against the stairwell wall, but Rasheed only tightened
his grip. One of her feet slipped off the step, and she
dropped her backpack between her legs so she could
grab the railing and keep from falling completely into
Rasheed's arms. She struggled to remove Rasheed's hands
from her hips, grabbing one of his fingers and yanking it
backward. Then, while moving her head back and forth
to make Eddie release her hair, she tried to push him
away.

Both Eddie and Rasheed seemed to be enjoying her
thrashing. Patrice twisted and turned wildly but suc-
ceeded only in getting her hair yanked harder. "Stop!" she
screamed. She could hear the sound echo in the hallway.

Tears began to well up in her eyes, but she knew she
shouldn't start crying. She knew that Eddie and Rasheed
would step up their harassment at any sign of weakness.

She managed to shove Eddie hard enough to move him back, but before she could do anything else he was in her face again.

"Yo, man! She don't want to show us what got Monty all sprung," whined Rasheed nastily. He tightened his grip on her hips and began squeezing them. "Don't she know that Monty shares all his women with us?"

"I'm not his woman!" snapped Patrice. "Don't touch me!"

"Oh, man, check it out," said Eddie. "She acting like she ain't been giving it up to my man."

"Hey, man, you think maybe our boy be lying to us about getting some of this?" said Rasheed. "That's cool, then *we* can break her in. You know, teach her a few things about being a *real* woman. Monty won't care," he added, sneering, "since she ain't his woman. Maybe he's just her little project. Making him all studious and crap." He laughed and pulled her even closer to him, enclosing her waist with his arm.

"I'm all about breaking ladies in, you know that!" answered Eddie. "She feel like she need to be broken in."

Rasheed's hand started creeping toward Patrice's groin. "Maybe I can be her next project when she's done with Monty. I'll start carrying around books and stuff, too."

That comment and the movement of Rasheed's hand

not only angered Patrice but terrified her, spurring her into furious action. She dug her fingernails deeply into Rasheed's forearm and scratched him as hard as she could. He squealed like a pig as his skin ripped under her fingernails. He released her in surprise and grabbed his injured arm. At that moment, she swept her backpack from between her feet and swung it upward with all her might, right between Eddie's legs. Eddie hollered and yanked his hand out of her hair, taking more than a few strands with it. He sank to the steps and curled into a ball, moaning.

Rasheed, unfortunately, wasn't as injured. He grabbed the backpack out of her hands and threw it down the stairwell. Then, apparently torn between wanting to get Patrice back in his clutches and wanting to help his friend, he was momentarily paralyzed. Patrice took advantage and quickly ran up the stairs, stepping on Eddie to get past him. She got to the tenth floor and flung the door open.

She stood shaking and leaning against the door. She could hear them cursing and laughing in the stairwell.

"Man, she a wildcat," hooted Rasheed. "She got you good."

"Yeah, well, I bet them scratches on your arm will scar up and you'll be reminded forever how you let her go. We could have had her, boy. With that hair done, she do look kinda good," replied Eddie, his voice sounding strained. "At least Monty is kicking us to the curb for a little hottie."

"Yeah, she be looking too much like that fine sister of hers," replied Rasheed. "I wouldn't mind a little of that, you know what I'm saying? I mean, they gotta be doing something 'cause we don't hardly see Monty no more."

Patrice heard them walking on the stairs now. But were they going up or down? She didn't wait to find out. She ran to apartment 1010 and pounded on the door. It swung open and Monty glared out, until he saw that it was Patrice. Seeing her distress, he backed out of the way and pulled her in.

"Hey, girl," he said. "What is it?"

Patrice stepped inside and began to cry.

• • •

It took a few minutes for Patrice to stop shaking and sobbing. Monty had led her to the couch and sat her down. He sat next to her, patiently waiting for her to calm down. But by the time she could think clearly, she began to wonder whether it was a good idea to tell Monty what had happened. After all, Rasheed and Eddie had said that Monty was telling lies about her and about their relationship. Would he be mad that she had told them the truth? Wouldn't he be more worried about his reputation and image than about hers? Why had he lied to them at all? Would Monty really say things like that about her? She shook her head, trying to clear it.

"Patrice. Patrice!" Monty looked at her, concern on his face. "What is going on?"

Patrice shook her head again before speaking. "Nothing," she lied. "I just—I don't know. Nothing."

Monty stared at her for a moment before speaking. "Nothing? You pound on my door, looking all freaked out, crying and stuff, and you say nothing is going on and I'm supposed to believe that? Who do I look like? BoBo the Fool?"

Patrice looked at Monty. "I got scared, that's all, and needed to get out of the stairwell."

"The stairwell? Scared by what?"

Patrice fell silent. She decided to play it safe for now. "Just this weird guy," she said, staring down at her feet. She couldn't look directly at Monty, see how worried he was about her, and tell him a lie.

Monty looked alarmed. "What guy? Did he touch you? Are you okay? Jesus, Patrice, we oughta call the police!"

"No!"

"No! No? Why no? What if you hadn't gotten away? What if you weren't near my floor? What if it had been Nefrititi instead of you?"

Patrice started crying again.

"Hey, stop, don't do that," Monty said gently, grabbing

a slightly used napkin off the floor and offering it to her. He slid closer.

Patrice took the napkin and wiped her eyes and blew her nose.

"Okay, what do you want to do?" he asked, obviously trying to sound calm.

"I want to go home," she said, trying not to sob.

"Okay, I'll walk you there." Monty stood up.

Patrice nodded. Even if he *had* said all those things, she didn't want to run into Eddie and Rasheed on the stairway again. She knew that with Monty around they would leave her alone. Patrice and Monty walked silently to the stairwell door.

"Oh no! My backpack!" she cried, remembering how Rasheed had thrown it down the stairs.

"Where is it?"

"It's on the staircase somewhere."

"Stay here. I'll make sure no one is there anymore."

Patrice nervously stood in the hall as Monty disappeared through the stairwell door. She could hear him on the stairs. Soon he returned and opened the door wide for her.

"Come on, there's no man in here."

"Is there—is there, um, anyone else?"

"No, 'Trice, it's completely empty. Really," he said, extending his hand.

She accepted his hand and felt calmed by his touch,

although now her stomach was all fluttery. They found her backpack a few steps down. Her books and papers were strewn up and down the staircase, many with footprints on them. She squatted to retrieve her stuff and noticed her essay papers.

Seeing her freshly typed essays torn and with a dirty sneaker footprint squarely in the middle of one of the pages brought new tears to her eyes.

Monty looked down at her and reached for her. She buried her face in his shoulder and sobbed some more.

9

AFTER A BAD NIGHT'S SLEEP, Patrice rose, very reluctantly, for school. Without thinking, she dressed in her baggiest jeans and her oldest sweatshirt. She absentmindedly pulled her hair back into a messy ponytail, and made absolutely sure that she wasn't alone when she went down the fifteen flights of stairs.

Blessedly, she made it all the way to school without an incident. She had walked so slowly that she had only enough time to shove her stuff into her locker and run to class.

She managed to get through the first half of the school day without seeing or hearing about Eddie or Rasheed. At lunch, however, Raven sat down beside Patrice, shoving aside the textbook she had been reading. "Hey, girl, what up?"

"Hello, Raven."

"Girl, I haven't told you how good your hair looked yesterday."

"Thanks, Raven."

"So why you got it back in that funky ponytail today?" Raven asked, eyeing the messy ponytail critically.

Patrice shrugged.

"So you and Monty still going strong, eh?"

Patrice looked at her. She was getting fed up. Sick of the unwanted attention, she figured the best she could do was to ignore Raven's prying questions. Patrice reached for her books and shrugged.

That didn't deter Raven one bit. "Of course, Eddie and Rasheed are telling people that you were trying to talk to them, too. Shoot, if I had Monty, I would be satisfied. I mean, he is too fine for words. But I guess you think you all that, huh?" Raven's voice had turned from sickeningly friendly to snide and nasty.

Patrice's face felt hot and her heart started beating fast. She glared at Raven and said through clenched teeth, "Raven, if you *must* know my business, Eddie and Rasheed are jackasses, and I wouldn't be caught dead with either one of them. As for Monty, we are friends. I don't care what you hear or from who. We are friends.

Which, by the way, is more than I can say for you and me. See ya, Raven."

Patrice slammed her book closed, gathered her things, and stormed out of the lunchroom, pleased, despite her anger, by the stunned look on Raven's face.

She headed to the computer room and quietly knocked on the door. Luckily, only the teacher was in the room and she let Patrice reprint her essays.

The rest of the school day people left her alone, much to her delight, and at the end of it she found Monty standing by her locker.

"I thought you'd want some company going home," he said.

Patrice smiled for the first time all day. She had been dreading the walk home and the possibility of running into Eddie and Rasheed in front of the building or, even worse, in the stairwell. Yet mixed with her relief was a touch of suspicion. How much of what Eddie and Rasheed had said about Monty was true? Could she trust Monty? Weren't Eddie and Rasheed better friends of his than she was? Monty did have a reputation when it came to girls—how much of that was true?

Thinking that she'd rather be safe than sorry, Patrice made a mental note not to become too close to Monty. After all, if she couldn't trust her own mother, why should she trust some boy she barely knew?

"Thanks, that would be great," said Patrice, closing

her locker and pulling on her coat. "I just need to talk with Mrs. Hutton real quick, 'kay?"

"Whatever."

Together they walked to the office. Monty leaned in his casual way against the office door, while Patrice walked in and asked the secretary for Mrs. Hutton. Mrs. Hutton poked her head out of her office and waved Patrice in.

"Hello there, Patrice. I'm glad you came by." Then, turning back to address Monty formally, she added, "Mr. Freeman, would you please join us? I've wanted to have a few words with you as well, and now is as good a time as any."

Monty looked surprised. He shoved his hands into his pockets and sort of sauntered into the office. He slumped down in the nearest chair, looking surly.

Patrice perched on the edge of her chair and, for some reason, felt extremely nervous.

"Let's see. First, Patrice. I've talked with the officials at Dogwood and they said having your aunt sign the form would be fine, as long as you get a copy of the guardianship papers and send them along with it."

Guardianship papers? Patrice had never thought of her aunt as her guardian. She and Cherise had just been dumped on her when their mother went to jail. She would ask her aunt as soon as possible.

Mrs. Hutton went on. "I've looked over the application. You've done an exceptional job with it, as expected. I look forward to reading your essays. As you know, I've gotten all of the recommendations, and I also have your transcripts ready to go. So, all I need is the parental permission and the essays. Here's the application back. Have your aunt sign on the parental-consent line, as well as write her social security number in the space indicated."

Patrice pulled the clean copies of the essays out of her backpack and handed them to Mrs. Hutton. She had intended to look them over one more time before showing them to her, but what the heck.

"Ah, you are so organized, Patrice. I'll read these and let you know if you need to make any corrections. Now, Mr. Freeman," she said, turning to Monty.

"Yeah." His voice sounded more than a little surly. At best, it was right on the edge of being disrespectful.

Patrice looked at him, a little surprised by his behavior.

"Recently, I've been hearing quite a lot about you from the teachers," Mrs. Hutton said coolly.

"Yeah. And?"

"It seems that your grades have soared in the past week or so. They say you have actually been turning in your homework. It is amazing how a little thing like simply doing homework can make an F student into an A one. I don't know what has caused this miraculous turn of events"—she glanced at Patrice—"but I hope it is a lasting change. You keep doing what you're doing and maybe *you'll* be able to win a scholarship in the competition next year. You've always been intelligent. You'd at least know someone at Dogwood, wouldn't he, Patrice?"

Patrice smiled and said, "I hope so, Mrs. Hutton." She glanced at Monty, who had stopped slumping in his seat and was sitting up straight. She couldn't decipher the look on his face, but at least it was no longer surly.

"Okay, that's it. You two go home and get going on your homework. Especially you, Mr. Freeman," she said with a wink and another glance toward Patrice.

They started on their way home, Monty taking Patrice's backpack. They walked along in silence.

"How you feeling?" asked Monty after a while.

"Okay."

"Did you see the man who messed with you today? You didn't tell me what he looked like."

Patrice looked down at her feet. She hated lying to Monty, but she still didn't know what he had said to his friends about them. She shrugged.

"Is that a yes or a no, Patrice?" he asked, sounding annoyed.

"It wasn't a man, it was Eddie and Rasheed," she blurted out, surprising both herself and Monty.

"What!"

"It wasn't a man," she repeated softly. "It was Eddie and Rasheed."

"Eddie and Rasheed was messing with you?" Monty snapped.

Patrice nodded and continued to look down at her feet.

Monty took hold of her arm and stopped her.

"Patrice, *look* at me."

Patrice slowly raised her head and looked at him, biting her lip. Her eyes began to tear up again.

"Eddie and Rasheed was messing with you? What they say to get you so upset?"

Patrice felt her face grow hot. "It wasn't just what they said," she answered softly, looking down again and noticing that the toes of her tennis shoes were wearing thin. She fell silent. She could feel him looking at her, waiting. She continued to study her shoes a few moments more before whispering, "It was also what they *did*."

"What they did? What did they do, Patrice? What happened?" he asked just as quietly, as if his speaking too loudly would scare her.

Patrice shrugged again. Her face felt hot. The whole thing was too embarrassing.

"What happened?" Monty asked again softly, but firmly. "Tell me."

Reluctantly, Patrice told him everything they had said, and all that they had done, in the stairwell.

When she finished, she peeked at Monty, who was silent. She could see the muscles in his jaw move and tighten as he clenched his teeth. He looked angry, even more than angry. She'd never seen him like this and it unnerved her a bit.

"Ain't none of what they said is true, 'Trice," he said through rigid jaws. "I would *never* say those things about you. What we have is too important to me. You ain't even like that. I know you didn't believe them. Right? You didn't buy that stuff, did you?"

Patrice finally looked up at him, but didn't answer. She *had* believed them and now she felt bad that she had. She should have let herself trust him.

" 'Trice, I did not say that. It was a lie. Well, okay, I am carrying around my books more."

She smiled at his last comment and began to feel relieved, as if a weight had been lifted from her shoulders. She nodded and looked at him, still smiling.

Satisfied, Monty was quiet for a minute, and they resumed walking. Then, sounding angry again, he said, "I told you we should have called the police."

"No, no, Monty. It's no big deal, really. It's over," said Patrice.

"Jesus, Patrice! They had their hands on you and had you cornered and you say it's no big deal! Hell, yeah, it's a big deal. They ain't got the right to treat you that way! Rasheed and Eddie are mostly talk, at least when they're apart. I mean, I thought they were. But they should never have touched you."

"Okay, Monty, I know, but there's not much I can do. Let's drop it, okay?" pleaded Patrice. She wanted to forget the whole thing.

"Patrice." Monty shook his head and stopped walking. "Yeah, well, you may not want to do anything, but wait until I see those two again. I know them better than you do. You get them together and it's like they urge each other on. Since you won't let the police teach them a lesson, I will."

Patrice didn't reply. She looked at Monty, who had started walking again, but she could still feel the anger radiating off him like heat. For the briefest of moments she had felt relieved. Telling Monty had made her feel lighter, better, less afraid. But seeing Monty's reaction, she found her old worries being replaced by a new one. She didn't know what Monty was going to do. Now she was more worried about him than she had ever been about running into Eddie and Rasheed again.

• • •

All through the homework session, Monty was quiet. He continued to look angry and fidgeted nervously, bouncing his leg up and down. He finished his math, but not in his usual ultra-neat manner. Patrice glanced at it surreptitiously and saw that while it was not neat, it was still correct.

Patrice was on edge herself. She suddenly felt uncomfortable around Monty, and quickly finished her work so she could hide in the kitchen while making dinner. The kids were amazingly quiet, doing their homework without their periodic whining—even Nefrititi. She figured they could feel the tension, because she sure could.

As Patrice was putting on water for spaghetti, Monty came into the kitchen and sat at the tiny table that barely fit opposite the stove.

"You know why they did that, don't you?" he asked finally, breaking the awkward silence.

Patrice shrugged. She hadn't thought too much about it. She was trying to think of anything but that.

"It's because you look so good with your hair fixed. Or at least you did. Eddie finally noticed how you really look. He could see your face and how pretty it is, since it wasn't halfway covered up by all that hair of yours, and Rasheed's just jealous."

Patrice felt her face get hot all over again and her stomach fill with butterflies. She didn't know whether to be thrilled by Monty's reaction to her looks, or appalled by the idea that something as simple as a new hairstyle could have made Eddie and Rasheed do what they did. She kept her back to Monty, and started to brown some hamburger meat for the cheap spaghetti sauce. As she cooked she thought about that day and what could have made Eddie and Rasheed act the way they did. She could only guess.

Finally, she said quietly, "Thank you, Monty. I mean

for the hair compliment. But I don't really care why they did it. Besides, I don't think it had to do with me or my hair. I think they hate that you have started to spend so much time with me. It's like they think I'm taking you from them or something. They aren't jealous of you, they are jealous of me. At least, that's what I think. It doesn't matter, though. I just don't want them to do it again."

"Don't worry. They won't. Trust that," muttered Monty angrily.

Something in his voice made Patrice turn around and look at him. "How do you know that?" she asked.

Monty looked at her with his usual intensity. "Believe me, 'Trice, they ain't gonna go there anymore. I'll make sure of that. Besides, really, I know you hate them and stuff, but they are mostly talk."

"Yeah, well, it wasn't just the talk that made me freak out, Monty. But, whatever. Let's drop it, okay? Don't do anything, 'kay?" Patrice looked at him for reassurance, but all she got was a single raised eyebrow. "Monty, really."

Monty didn't answer. Patrice turned back to the meat, worry clawing at her stomach again.

The rest of the night was quiet. The mood remained somber, and Patrice was relieved when Monty and Michael left for their own apartment after dinner. Marc-Anthony and Nefrititi didn't even go through the usual fighting about whose turn it was to take the first bath.

Patrice stayed up later than usual, waiting for her aunt

to get home from her waitressing. Finally, at a quarter to one, Patrice heard her aunt turning the key in the door.

"Girl, what you still doing up? You know better—it's a school night. Whoa, we were so busy tonight. I made good tips, but I'm gonna be dead tomorrow! You should be in bed."

"I know, but I wanted to ask you something, Auntie," said Patrice, stifling a yawn.

Her aunt collapsed on the couch and began pulling off her boots. "What is it?"

"Um, for the application to Dogwood. I need a copy of the guardianship papers and your signature on the form."

"The guardianship papers? Girl, is you crazy?" said Auntie Mae with a laugh.

"Why? What?"

"Girl, we ain't rich. What make you think we got guardianship papers? NaNa got her trifling butt thrown in jail, and you came to live here. End of story. What kind of papers we need for that? Only rich people got guardianship papers. Some lawyer came up to me at the sentencing, asking if I wanted him to draw up them papers. I asked him why I need them and he started talking about wills and money and stuff, like NaNa got money to leave y'all. I told him I'd call him, but I never did. I ain't got money to pay for that."

Patrice's heart sank, even though she wasn't surprised. Without the papers, her aunt couldn't sign the application and that meant she somehow *had* to get to Mount Rose and to the women's prison for her mother's signature. How could she rely on Cherise to get her there? Sometimes Cherise came through, but most of the time she didn't. But it seemed that Patrice didn't have any other choice. Auntie Mae didn't have a car—as far as Patrice knew, she didn't even know how to drive. Besides, Auntie Mae worked more than sixty hours a week and Patrice knew how tired she was. It didn't seem fair to give her yet another chore.

"That why you waited so long for me tonight?" asked Auntie Mae, taking out a cigarette and lighting it.

"Yes, ma'am," Patrice answered quietly.

"Guess you wasted your time. Girl, you coulda been asleep." Auntie Mae yawned. "Go on to bed."

"Yes, ma'am."

Just when she thought things were falling into place, everything seemed to be falling apart. Patrice walked slowly down the hall and crawled into bed. She tossed and turned, trying to figure out what to do.

She considered asking Mrs. Hutton for help, but the thought made her sick to her stomach with embarrassment. She didn't think she could ask her principal for a lift to the prison to visit her mom.

Each solution she thought of made her sadder and sadder. When she finally drifted off to sleep, her pillow was wet with tears.

10

AFTER SUCH A LATE NIGHT, Patrice woke up feeling tired, cranky, and as if the whole world was on her shoulders. She dragged herself out of bed and hastily put on whatever clothes she could find. The ponytail was back again. Wanting to give Auntie Mae an extra fifteen minutes of sleep, she got MarcAnthony and Nefrititi ready and off to school. She was relieved that the elevator was finally working.

All the way to school, Patrice thought about the application. She had no idea where her father was. Even when she had lived in Georgia with his mother, she hadn't seen him more than a couple of times. All she knew was that he was in the military. The last she'd heard, he was somewhere overseas.

Maybe she should sign the form herself. But what if they somehow found out that she had forged her mother's signature? They certainly wouldn't give her a scholarship. She didn't want to take any risks. She wanted to do the whole thing right. But in order to do that, she would have to find some way to Mount Rose. She knew it wasn't all that far. It was a little more than an hour away, maybe sixty, seventy miles at the most, but for a thirteen-year-old that was far enough—too far to ride a bike, even if she had one. The subway didn't go way out there; neither did the city bus. Suddenly it dawned on her. Greyhound! That's how she could get there, by Greyhound bus. She wondered how much it would cost and whether she had enough money in her piggy bank.

Patrice was in such deep thought that she didn't notice that she was approaching school. More important, she didn't notice the people standing in front of the door until she heard their voices.

"Well, look who's here, Rasheed," sneered Eddie, startling Patrice.

"Our little wildcat from the other day," answered Rasheed. The rest of the boys snickered and guffawed. Rasheed and Eddie had obviously told them their version of what had happened.

Patrice stopped in her tracks. Her eyes darted over the group. Monty wasn't anywhere in sight. She gripped her backpack tightly and took a step back.

"Oh, baby, don't leave us," said Rasheed, walking toward her.

"Yeah," added Eddie, "we got some unfinished business."

The gang of boys hooted, crowding closer, forming a circle around the three of them, trying to get a better view.

Patrice's heart was beating a mile a minute. This time there were too many of them.

"Leave me alone," she said, surprised by the strength of her voice.

"That's right, fellas, back off," added a voice from behind her.

Patrice felt her body flood with relief as she turned around to see Monty walking casually up to the group.

"You ain't in charge of nothing no more, Monty," said Eddie weakly. Obviously, he didn't want to back down immediately, especially in front of the whole gang.

Rasheed nodded in agreement, but kept his mouth shut. He reached out and grabbed Patrice's arm.

"Stop!" shouted Patrice, yanking her arm from his grip. "Don't touch me!"

"Man, I ain't gonna tell you again. Leave her alone." Monty's voice was low and menacing.

"Why? You want to keep this fresh thing all to yourself?" sneered Rasheed. But he backed up, taking a step away from Patrice and Monty, who was now in the inner circle, standing slightly in front of Patrice. "What makes Puffy so damn special? Hell, you ain't got no time for nobody these days except her. You need to let us see what got you so wigged out."

Monty took a step toward Eddie, who backed up behind Rasheed. Rasheed reached out and poked the books that Monty had been carrying out of his hands. They scattered on the ground. The gang of boys muttered excitedly, anxious to see what would happen next.

"Maybe he becoming all high and mighty like Puffy, y'all." Eddie laughed. "Hell, every time I see this fool now, he got some books. You think you too good for us now? Too smart?"

Monty turned slowly toward Eddie and without another word punched him squarely in the nose. A second later, he turned, took a quick step toward Rasheed, and punched him dead in his left eye.

"Ahh! Man, we was just jokin'!" said Rasheed, bending over and cupping his hand over his eye. All pretense of toughness was gone. "You didn't have to hit me, Monty. You wrong!"

The rest of the boys backed up quickly, anxious to get out of Monty's reach and back on his good side.

"From now on, leave Patrice alone. You understand?" Monty said quietly to Rasheed, who looked at him with his one good eye, and to Eddie, who was holding his head back as far as he could, his hand trying to stop the trickle of blood from his nose. "I said, do you understand?" repeated Monty quietly, his voice soft, but somehow still threatening.

Rasheed nodded.

"Yeah, man," whined Eddie. His voice was more nasal than usual, since he was now pinching his nose with his fingers.

"That goes for all of you. Don't talk *to* her. Don't talk *about* her. And *don't* touch her. Don't even think about getting close enough to touch her. Don't even *look* at her. Got it? You so much as look her way, y'all gotta answer to me. All right?"

His speech was met with a chorus of *yeah*'s, *cool*'s, and *bet*'s from the rest of the boys, who probably wanted desperately to laugh at Rasheed and Eddie, but even more not to anger Monty.

Just then the door burst open and Mrs. Hutton came out.

"Exactly *what* is going on here, gentlemen . . . and lady?" she asked, looking unhappily around the group. "What is so riveting that you seem not to have heard the bell for first period?"

No one said a word. Monty was looking unblinkingly at Mrs. Hutton, while Rasheed and Eddie were still nursing their wounds, looking everywhere but at the angry principal or Patrice.

"Surely none of you would have the nerve to be fighting right in front of my office window," she said, waving her arm toward the window only a couple of feet away from where the fight had taken place. "Mr. Walters, what exactly happened to your eye? Mr. Brooks, is your nose actually bleeding?" she asked incredulously.

They both glanced quickly at Monty, but shrugged and said nothing.

"Mr. Freeman, do you have any idea why Mr. Brooks is bleeding and why Mr. Walters' eye seems to be getting puffier by the minute?"

"Yeah," Monty answered in the same surly tone he had used the previous day. "Sure do."

"Well?" asked Mrs. Hutton, clearly out of patience.

"I hit them," he answered with a shrug.

"I see," replied Mrs. Hutton. "Mr. Walters, Mr. Brooks, go to the nurse's office and get fixed up, then go on to class. Mr. Freeman, follow me, please. The rest of you, get to your classes *now*."

She spun on her heels and entered the school. Monty strolled after her, walking as if he didn't have a care in the world. Rasheed and Eddie trotted off to the nurse's office like wounded puppies. The rest of the boys filed silently into the school, leaving Patrice standing alone.

She started walking slowly toward her class, but knew she couldn't abandon Monty. She turned and headed quickly for the principal's office.

"Hello, Patrice," said Mrs. Hutton's secretary. "You can't talk with Mrs. Hutton at the moment. She's with a student right now. You'll have to come back after school."

"But, Mrs. Logan, it's really important that I talk to her right now!" pleaded Patrice.

"Sorry," answered Mrs. Logan. "You'll have to wait until after school. Go on to class now; first period started more than five minutes ago."

As soon as Mrs. Logan looked away, Patrice headed for the principal's office. Mrs. Logan saw her, but before she could chastise her again, Patrice had reached the principal's office and flung open the door. "Mrs. Hutton!"

Mrs. Hutton and Monty looked at her. Both appeared startled by her sudden appearance.

"Patrice, whatever it is that you have to say will have to wait until after school," said Mrs. Hutton tersely.

"No, it can't," said Patrice quietly.

Mrs. Hutton looked up, her face showing extreme irritation.

"Patrice, you have more than three weeks to get the application in," she began. "Whatever you need will have to—"

"It has nothing to do with Dogwood Academy, Mrs. Hutton," interrupted Patrice, taking a step inside the office. "It's why Monty was fighting. It was my fault," she said in a rush. "I'm to blame."

"Really?" Mrs. Hutton's eyebrows shot up in surprise. "And how is that? Did you take his arm and make him hit them?"

"Well, no, but, he was—Rasheed—Eddie—" she stammered.

"A complete, coherent sentence would be nice, Ms. Williams," replied Mrs. Hutton curtly.

Patrice took a deep breath.

"Monty hit Rasheed and Eddie because they were, um, messing with me the other day and then again today. He was protecting me," she said in a rush.

" 'Messing with'?" asked Mrs. Hutton, sitting upright in her chair, her expression slowly changing from anger to concern. "What exactly do you mean by 'messing with'?"

Patrice sighed and set her backpack on the floor. It seemed she would have to tell the story again.

"The other day, Rasheed and Eddie cornered me in the stairwell of our apartment building and were touching me, um, inappropriately. Then today when I tried to get into school, they started up again. Monty told them to stop, but they wouldn't listen, so he hit them. For me."

Mrs. Hutton's eyes grew wide. She looked at Monty now. "Is that correct, Mr. Freeman?"

"Yeah," Monty answered with a shrug.

"Well, that changes everything," said Mrs. Hutton softly. "Mr. Freeman, forget about the weeklong suspension we were discussing before we were interrupted. Go on to class. But next time please try to convince them with your voice and not your fists. You have excellent leadership skills, Monty," she added as he rose to his feet. "Always try to employ those skills before using your fists."

Monty's surly look changed immediately to one of surprise. "Yeah, okay."

She reached over to the phone. "Nurse Hanna, have you finished with Rasheed Walters and Eddie Brooks yet? Well, when you *are* finished, please send them to my office."

Monty was strolling out of the door, and Patrice had turned to follow him.

"Patrice, I need to speak with you further," said Mrs. Hutton.

Patrice, who no longer felt bold, shuddered. *Now what?* she thought. "Yes, ma'am," she said softly.

"Close the door."

Patrice shut the door and stood clutching her backpack, desperately wishing she was in her first-period class.

"Have a seat," said Mrs. Hutton.

"Yes, ma'am."

"Are you all right?" asked Mrs. Hutton gently.

"Yes, ma'am."

"Patrice, I need to decide whether I should report this to the police. I need to know exactly what happened. I need to know how they touched you."

"Oh, Mrs. Hutton, do we have to?" Patrice was suddenly on the verge of tears. She just wanted to forget about everything that had happened. Why couldn't she go on with her life?

"Yes. We do," replied Mrs. Hutton. "We have to impress upon Rasheed and Eddie that such behavior is not only inappropriate, but illegal as well. It's called assault, and depending on where they touched you, it could be sexual assault. They must learn *now* that such action cannot be taken lightly. What if they try it with someone else? Someone who doesn't have a Monty for a friend?"

A single, hot tear ran down Patrice's cheek. She wiped it away quickly and nodded. Mrs. Hutton pulled out a notepad and pen from her desk.

"They cornered me in the stairwell at the apartment building and Eddie ran his hand through my hair and Rasheed had his hands on my hips and around my waist. He started to move his hand down, you know, down." Patrice inclined her head toward her groin. Mrs. Hutton grimaced and nodded. "But I scratched Rasheed and hit Eddie in the—in his private place—with my backpack. Then I ran up to Monty's apartment and he walked me home. Today, Rasheed grabbed me by the arm, but that's all," blurted out Patrice.

Mrs. Hutton breathed a sigh of relief. "So they didn't get under your clothes or touch your private parts?"

"No, ma'am."

"Good. What were they saying while they did all this?"

Patrice felt her face get hot again. She squirmed in her seat. This was as hard as telling Monty.

"Well, Rasheed said they could teach me a few things about being a woman. He and Eddie said I felt ripe and needed to be broken in. Stuff like that."

Mrs. Hutton drew a sharp breath. "I see."

She wrote out a tardy pass with Patrice's name on it.

"That will do for now, Patrice. Go on to class. Try not to worry about anything. Try to concentrate on getting good grades so we can get you into Dogwood."

"Yes, ma'am," Patrice answered, thinking, *Fat chance without my mom's signature.* Maybe she *should* tell Mrs. Hutton the trouble she was having. She opened her mouth to say something, then thought, *What could Mrs. Hutton possibly do to help?* Besides, she was tired of relying on people to get her out of jams. Look what had happened to Monty. She decided to go with the Greyhound plan. So she swallowed her question and rose to leave.

She grabbed her backpack and opened the door to find Rasheed and Eddie in the outer office. Both smirked at her. They obviously thought it was she and Monty who were in trouble. They quickly put on their pitiful, injured, and innocent looks before walking into the principal's office.

11

PATRICE FELT ANXIOUS for the rest of the day and could barely concentrate in class. After school she rushed to her locker, hoping to find Monty there. She didn't know what she would say to him, but she wanted them to still be friends. He had stood up for her in front of a lot of people and had almost gotten into a lot of trouble because of it. She felt she owed him something. She just didn't know what.

"Hey, 'Trice," Monty greeted her.

Her stomach flipped when she turned the corner and saw him leaning against her locker, in his normal cool stance, talking with Chanterelle and Sarah.

"Hi, Monty," Patrice answered with a shy smile.

Chanterelle and Sarah seemed miffed to have lost Monty's attention so quickly, but didn't say anything.

"Hi, Chanterelle. Hi, Sarah," Patrice said politely. She tried to think of something else to say to them, but nothing came to mind, so she simply smiled at them and turned to get her things out of her locker.

"Monty," said Chanterelle, "me and Sarah is heading to the corner store. Wanna come?"

"Nah," answered Monty.

"Oh, come on, Monty," said Sarah, batting her eyes at him. "It'll be a lot more fun than anything you could do with her."

Monty laughed and Patrice felt her stomach tighten, but didn't say anything.

"I doubt it," Monty replied with his smirk. "You ready, 'Trice?" he asked, turning away from the stunned-looking girls.

Patrice smiled at him. "Yep," she answered happily.

"Cool. See y'all later," Monty said to Chanterelle and Sarah.

"Bye!" Patrice said softly, unable to stop grinning.

She and Monty walked off.

Once they were out of earshot, Patrice turned to Monty with a smile. "You know, you could have gone with them."

"I know that. Did you want me to go with them?"

To her surprise she answered quickly, "Absolutely not."

Monty laughed and grabbed her backpack.

They walked in silence.

"You don't happen to know how much it costs to take the Greyhound to Mount Rose, do you?" asked Patrice, more out of a wish to break the silence than anything else.

"Nah, I don't even know where Mount Rose is. Why?"

" 'Cause I've got to get my mother to sign the Dogwood application, and I don't think I can depend on Cherise to get me there in time. I want to give the forms to Mrs. Hutton. I just want to finish them."

"When you gonna go?"

"I don't know. Soon. I've got a little over three weeks before I have to turn in everything."

"Sounds like plenty of time to me. Anyway, why don't you just sign it for her?"

"I thought about that, but I'd be too nervous that they would somehow find out. Plus it asks for her social security number, and I have no idea what it is. Besides, I want to do everything right and not have to lie and stuff, you know?"

"You always this honest?"

"Yes, I guess so. I'm not real good at lying. Will your friends be mad at you for hitting Eddie and Rasheed?"

She had meant to avoid the whole issue, but the question had slipped out.

"Don't know. Doubt it, though. They like seeing a fight. I don't care one way or the other. Most of them is weak. Spending their time picking on people who can't, or won't, defend themselves. They are just trying to act bad in front of the group, that's all."

"You know, the drug dealers who hang around don't bother me as much as your friends do—or did."

Monty looked at her and nodded. He continued to look at her closely, studying her, before speaking again. "Yeah, at least for now they don't. You still look young enough to them that they won't try and hook up with you, but that won't last much longer. Eddie and them pick on you 'cause they don't understand you and because you cry and run away. You're easy pickin's. Those older dudes is too concerned about running drugs and making money to worry about you. At least right now."

Patrice shuddered. "I hope I get one of those scholarships," she said, more to herself than to Monty.

"Yeah, me, too. I guess."

"You guess!" Patrice said teasingly. "What, you want one instead of me, Mr. Perfect Math Paper?"

Monty chuckled. "Nah, it's just that I'll miss you and your weird ways, that's all."

"Weird? I'm not weird. Why do you think I'm weird?" Patrice demanded with mock outrage.

"You is weird. You always got your head in some book. All you do is study. You ain't like the other girls, getting your hair done and shoplifting clothes to wear. Look how you dress! I ain't never seen Chanterelle and Sarah in old jeans and faded sweatshirts. Cain't nobody even tell how you're shaped or nothing in all that."

"How I'm shaped? Who cares about my shape anyway?" Patrice shouted with a hoot of laughter.

Monty grinned. "Oh, I know a few people who would like to see you in something less baggy."

Patrice snorted, not believing him. "Yeah, right. So I guess I am weird. So why are you hanging out with such a freak?"

Monty turned and looked at her directly. The lightness of the conversation evaporated instantly. "Because, weirdo, I like you. You're real. It's like you're the only clean thing around here."

"Oh." It was all Patrice could think of to say.

They walked in silence a few steps before Monty spoke again. "You know that empty lot near school?"

"Yeah, why?"

"Well, the whole lot is filled with junk and trash and crap, but last spring, in the middle of the trash this flower bloomed. This pretty little flower, right there, in the middle of a lot full of garbage. It was the weirdest thing. I mean, where did it come from? I didn't know whether to pick it or let it keep growing. I'd go by there every day to look at that stupid flower 'cause it was so unique and pretty and it tripped me out that it could bloom in the middle of all that trash. Then one day I went by and someone had thrown an old stuffed chair over it and broke it. Killed it. I told myself that the next time I saw something beautiful trying to survive in the middle of trash I'd do what I could to protect it, to make sure it grew and that nobody messed it up. So, I guess you're my flower."

Patrice stared at him. "Wow," she said softly. "Wow. I— Thank you, Monty."

Monty looked at her and smiled. "Hey, no problem. My pleasure."

. . .

As soon as she got home and got MarcAnthony and Nefrititi settled, Patrice grabbed the yellow pages and looked up Greyhound Lines. She called and found out that the ride would be about an hour long and would cost twenty-four dollars round-trip. She would have to go from Chicago to Joliet, then catch a city bus out to the correctional facility in Mount Rose. She was pretty sure she had at least thirty dollars in her piggy bank, but she would be wiping it out, at least until her next birthday, when her grandma would send her a crisp new twenty-dollar bill. She had enough for one round-trip.

The Greyhound bus left at ten-thirty in the morning

and arrived at Joliet at eleven-forty. She had no idea how she was going to get from the bus station to the city bus, but surely there was only one bus to Mount Rose, Illinois. The bus back to Chicago didn't leave until six thirty-five p.m., so not only did she have plenty of time to talk with her mother, she had *too* much time. She really didn't have much choice, though.

It was already January 23, which meant she had twenty-four days to get to Mount Rose. She wanted to do it as soon as possible, so she decided to go that coming weekend. After checking her piggy bank, she saw that she had exactly $31.65. Enough to get there and back, plus a little extra in case she needed something while she was there. Just thinking about going to the prison to talk with her mother made her palms sweat and her heart beat fast. She hadn't really gotten the chance to know her mother before she had been carted off to jail.

While Patrice was with her grandmother in Georgia, the only thing she had gotten from her mother was a photograph of her with Cherise and Marquis, and a couple of birthday, Christmas, and Easter cards. Then one day, out of the blue, Patrice arrived home from school to find her mother sitting in the living room.

Her grandmother had been there, looking angry. Her mother had worn a beautiful navy suit and looked so professional and flawless that Patrice had been a bit starstruck. In the one picture she had of her, her mother had simply looked pretty, but in person she was beautiful. Then her mother had started the lying, talking about how much she wanted to raise Patrice and how Patrice needed to be with her mother and siblings. It all sounded so good: how well she was doing, how much money she made at her fancy job, and how she could afford to keep Patrice and send her to the best schools in the city.

Her grandmother had looked skeptical, but Patrice knew that her grandmother was getting older. She had started to complain about ever-increasing aches and pains. She was having trouble driving at night and had pretty much stopped driving at all, unless it was absolutely necessary. Patrice did whatever she could to help out, but there was a limit to how much a middle-school kid could do. With a lot of tears, Patrice had been packed up and sent off with her mother the very next day.

As Patrice and her mother drove from Georgia to Illinois, the scenery outside the car window turned from green to brown, the sky from blue to gray, the weather from warm to cold. By the time they got to Chicago, Patrice had gone from a sunny 70-degree Tuesday in Vidalia, Georgia, to a chilly 40-degree Wednesday in Chicago. She hadn't had proper clothes for the weather, and had been given some of Cherise's old sweats. It seemed she'd been in old sweats and assorted hand-me-downs ever since.

Within days of her arrival in Chicago, Patrice knew

the show her mother had put on in Georgia was a little charade to lure her away. Patrice saw that not only did her mother not have the kind of job, or the kind of money, she had bragged about in her grandmother's living room, not even the elegant suit was hers. Through overheard conversations, Patrice learned that the reason she'd been brought to Chicago was to help get her mother out of trouble.

Unfortunately, that hadn't worked, and two months after picking up Patrice in Georgia, her mother had been taken to jail, sentenced to eight to ten years for identity theft and welfare fraud. Patrice hadn't seen much of her, except once or twice in the courtroom, since that day. Now the only communication between them was the cards Patrice got on her birthday and Christmas, and the cards she sent on Christmas, Mother's Day, and her mother's birthday.

With a sigh and a shrug, Patrice shook herself out of her reverie and put up dinner, then did the last bit of reading for her homework. There was no way she could let her mother know she was coming on such short notice, but it wasn't as if her mother was going to be busy or on a trip or something, so Patrice didn't think any more of it.

The rest of the week went smoothly. There was still no sign of Eddie and Rasheed, not even around the building. Patrice was a bit scared to ask what had happened to them, so she resolved not to say anything and to enjoy the peace their absence brought. She and Monty had gotten into the habit of walking to and from school together, and the walk was no longer so cold or lonely— or frightening. She'd stopped counting blocks altogether. Michael was doing extremely well and seemed to be a much happier, more outgoing kid. Soon she wouldn't need to tutor him at all. Life seemed pretty good.

On Friday, she made a point of making a big tuna casserole, so that there would be leftovers for Saturday. The bus did not return until nearly eight at night, and Patrice knew her aunt might be a little peeved if she had to make dinner herself. Auntie Mae didn't mind how late Patrice stayed out, as long as her chores were done and food was prepared. Patrice knew that her aunt cared for her, but she also knew how much Auntie Mae had begun to depend on her. To make sure she would have enough time in the morning, Patrice stayed up late on Friday getting as many of her chores done as possible.

Saturday morning she got up extremely early. By nine o'clock, Patrice had finished her chores, made a big breakfast, and cleaned the kitchen. Fifteen minutes later, on her way out the door, Patrice said that she'd be home late. Her aunt grunted an acknowledgment from her favorite spot on the couch.

Before leaving the building, Patrice made sure that she had all the necessary papers. It was a little more than a half hour's walk to the bus station. She could have taken the subway or the city bus, but she wanted to save all her money for the trip.

Patrice was so focused on her mission that she didn't even see Monty and his brothers in the park until she was almost past it. Monty waved her over, but since she wanted to be on time for the bus, she said she'd talk to him later and went on her way.

Monty's curiosity must have gotten the better of him, because, ignoring his brothers' shouts, he walked with her for half a block. "The library is the other way," he teased.

"Yeah, well, your brothers and the park are, too," she answered.

"Where are you going this warm winter day?" he asked.

"Warm! You Northerners think because it warms up to forty-three in the middle of January, you're having a heat wave. I gotta go see my mom. You'd better get back to your brothers."

Monty nodded. He stopped at the light with her and grinned. "Well, maybe you have a little more guts than I thought. See ya later." He turned and jogged back to the park, and Patrice, enjoying the rare winter sun on her face, continued to the bus station.

12

IT WAS ABOUT ELEVEN FORTY-FIVE by the time Patrice stepped off the bus and looked around the station. Searching for someone to tell her which local bus to take to the prison, she couldn't see anyone in an official uniform. She tried not to panic and assessed her situation. She had seven dollars and some change in her pocket. With luck, she could get to and from the prison on that. Only one other person had gotten off in Joliet with her—an elderly lady with a bag full of knitting. Patrice watched her as she crossed the street and sat at a bus stop. Summoning her courage, she walked over to the lady and asked if she had any idea how to get to Mount Rose Women's Correctional Center.

"Why, that's where I'm heading, sweetie," said the

woman kindly. "There's a bus that comes in about every thirty minutes. It takes you right to the prison's visitors' entrance."

Patrice felt relieved. So far, the trip was going very well. "How much is the bus ride there?"

"Oh, it's only a dollar and a half each way," said the woman. "Who are you going to see?"

Patrice felt embarrassed, but answered, "My mother."

"I'll be seeing my daughter. I've about finished this here blanket for her. She says the nights can be so cold in there. I don't get to see her too often, and I like to bring her a little something each time I come."

Patrice hadn't thought to bring anything for her mother. She had no idea what her mother might need.

She sat on the end of the bench, and soon the bus arrived. Thirty minutes later, it stopped in front of a sprawling beige building surrounded by a fence topped with coils of barbed wire. She and the woman got off the bus, and Patrice followed the woman into a building that sat just in front of the main prison building.

The room was small and chilly. There were a dozen plastic chairs, a single pop machine, a window, and a door. The handful of people in the room sat looking expectantly at the door, which appeared to lead to the prison.

Patrice watched as the woman went up to the window and wrote something on a clipboard. The guard behind the bulletproof glass took the form the lady slid to her and told the woman to have a seat.

Patrice stepped up and took the clipboard with a blank form. It looked simple enough to fill out. She wrote her name, her mother's, and the date, and signed the form. The only space she left blank was her mother's prison number. She had never heard of a prison number. She slid the form under the glass and waited. The guard took the paper and glanced at it before looking up at her with an annoyed expression on her face.

"You need the prisoner's number," the guard snapped. She shoved the form back under the glass to Patrice.

"I don't know it," admitted Patrice.

The guard sighed loudly and looked even more annoyed. "What relation are you to the prisoner?" she asked.

"Her daughter," answered Patrice.

"Hmph," snorted the guard. "Fine, you'll have to wait while I look up the prisoner's number. Sit down."

A few minutes went by and the door opened. A guard called out a couple of names, and the people who had been waiting got up and followed her through the door. A few more minutes went by and the same guard appeared and called out another name. The woman who had helped Patrice looked over and smiled at her before following the guard.

Fifteen minutes went by, then half an hour. During that time, a few more people had trickled in, and all of them had been called and had followed the guard through the door. Finally, summoning her courage, Patrice went back up to the window.

"Um, excuse me, ma'am."

"Yeah, what?"

"I've been here for almost an hour and I still haven't been called."

The guard looked at her as if she'd never seen her before.

"Did you fill out a form?"

"Yes, ma'am," answered Patrice. Then she added, "I didn't have my mother's prisoner number, remember?"

A small flicker of recognition shot through the guard's eyes. "Oh yeah. Here, fill out the form again. I'll look up the number."

So Patrice filled out the form again, slipped it under the glass, and went back to her seat.

At last, the door opened. Patrice's heart did a flip. *This is it!* she thought. The guard called her name and Patrice stood up, but the guard closed the door behind her and walked over to where Patrice was sitting.

"You here to see Shanice Renée Brown?" she asked, looking at the form Patrice had filled out.

"Yes, ma'am."

"You ain't on her visitor list."

"Her visitor list?"

The guard sighed. She spoke slowly, as if Patrice were a nitwit. "You are not on her visitor list. Each prisoner has a list of people that are approved to visit and you ain't on hers."

Patrice's heart sank to her feet. "So I can't see her, even for a little?" she asked, trying, and failing, to keep the whining tone out of her voice. She blinked her eyes several times to stop tears from forming.

"No. You ain't on her visitor list," the guard repeated. "You gotta be on her visitor list to see her."

Despite her efforts, Patrice's eyes began to fill with tears. The guard noticed and dropped a bit of her cold demeanor.

"She your mama?"

"Yes, ma'am," answered Patrice, her voice just barely audible.

"Okay, what you need to do is write your mama and tell her to put your name on her visitor list. And then you can come anytime to see her. Besides, visiting time is nine a.m. to one forty-five daily, holidays included. It's over."

"Yes, ma'am. Thank you," said Patrice, wiping away a stray tear.

After all the time she'd spent traveling and waiting, she had only what she'd come with: a blank section on her Dogwood application. And she was minus almost thirty dollars.

The door suddenly opened. Patrice's heart leaped; maybe they would let her say hi. But instead of the guard, all the people who had been called before her came streaming in.

Patrice pulled a notebook out of her bag and quickly wrote a note to her mother, saying that she wanted to see her and would she please, *please* put Patrice's name on her visitor list. She went back to the little window and knocked.

"Didn't Annette tell you that you couldn't see your mama today?" snapped the guard.

"Yes. I was wondering if you could deliver this letter to my mother for me."

"What I look like, the post office? All letters got to go to the central processing unit before the prisoners get them."

Patrice started to turn away, then boldly turned back. "Well, do you have an envelope and the address, please?" she asked politely but firmly.

The guard sighed yet again and walked off, muttering something under her breath.

She returned with an envelope and an address torn from a piece of letterhead stationery.

"I ain't got no stamps," she said sarcastically, pushing the envelope and scrap paper under the window toward Patrice. She then pulled the shade down abruptly.

Patrice grinned in spite of herself. "Thank you so much," she said to the shade.

She turned to go and wait for the bus, when the shade popped up with a snap.

"Hey! Be sure you put the prisoner's number on the second line of the address, along with her name."

Patrice turned back. "Um, I don't—" she started.

The guard grunted. A few seconds later she slid a second piece of scrap paper under the window. She then pulled the shade down again.

On the paper was a bunch of numbers.

Patrice sighed and went to wait for the bus.

By two thirty-five, Patrice was sitting in the bus station in Joliet. The bus to Chicago didn't leave until six thirty-five, so she had a lot of time on her hands. She decided that since she had to mail the letter anyway, she might as well write a real letter to her mother. So she took out her notebook and wrote a three-page letter explaining exactly why she needed to see her. She added what little gossip she knew about her mother's brothers and sisters, as well as what she knew about Cherise and Marquis, which wasn't much.

Finally, she put the letter in the envelope, carefully addressed it, and walked to the little post office, which she had seen from the bus. She bought a single stamp from the vending machine and mailed the letter right there.

Somehow, in the next three weeks, she had to earn another thirty dollars and get back to Mount Rose.

Patrice slowly walked to the Joliet bus station, the winter wind blowing strongly in her face. As she sat waiting for the bus pretending to read a book, she was trying to figure out how she was going to get enough money to return.

• • •

On the ride back to Chicago, Patrice stared blankly out of the window. Every so often, a tear would slide down her cheek, which she would quickly wipe away. Thirty dollars. How was she ever going to earn thirty dollars in three weeks? Each time she thought about the money, her eyes would fill with tears. There was no way she would ask her aunt for it. It was too much money. All she could think of was to ask Cherise for the money, although she couldn't rely on Cherise for anything. But what choice did she have? She would have to promise to give Cherise the gift money from her grandmother. There was no way Cherise would sacrifice a Saturday, her busiest, most profitable day, or a Sunday, her precious day off, to drive Patrice. She just had to ask her sister for money. Patrice sighed. She remembered the last conversation she'd had with Cherise. Most of it was about how Cherise didn't have any money to give to Marquis.

After a long, sad ride, the bus finally pulled up to the station. Patrice had just left the building when someone grabbed her arm from behind. She let out a scream and yanked it away.

"Yo, 'Trice. Calm down, girl, it's just me."

She turned to see Monty standing there. "What are you doing here?" she asked.

"Waiting for you," he said simply.

"Waiting for me?"

"That's what I said, isn't it? Waiting for you."

"Why?"

"Because it's too dark for you to be walking home from the bus depot alone. Because you was gone all day and I was beginning to worry about you. Because I want to. That's why."

Patrice smiled shyly at him. "Thanks, Monty."

"No prob. How'd it go?"

Patrice didn't really want to tell Monty about her day. She really didn't want to tell anyone about her day. It was too depressing and way too embarrassing. But he had been waiting and he had been worried about her. It was the very least she could do.

So during the cold, dark walk home Patrice described her day. By the end of the story, she, of course, was crying.

"Hey, Patrice, don't cry. It will all work out."

"How, Monty?" She stood shivering and sobbing outside their building.

" 'Cause it will," replied Monty without a trace of

doubt in his voice. "Besides, you know, you cry *a lot*. You gotta stop."

"I know. I can't help it," answered Patrice.

"Really, 'Trice, it will all work out. I promise. Stop crying."

Patrice looked at him and nodded numbly, not really believing it. The hope she had of leaving Chicago and going to a wonderful school was beginning to fade. On noticing that the ELEVATOR BROKEN sign had reappeared, she sighed such a deep sigh that Monty looked at her with concern.

"Really, Patrice, thirty bucks ain't that much. We'll figure it out."

The only thing that lightened Patrice's heart in that statement was the word *we*. She liked being part of a "we."

Monty walked Patrice up to her aunt's apartment and then went down to his own. Patrice felt her stomach growl. She hadn't eaten all day, but knowing her aunt, there wasn't going to be much of a meal left for her.

Patrice went into the kitchen. Sure enough, there was only a little tuna casserole left. So she quickly boiled a hot dog and ate it with some slightly stale chips. It was fine. Her aunt and cousins were engrossed in a made-for-TV movie and barely said more than hi to her, which was fine, too. She wasn't in the mood to talk anyway.

After a long, hot bath, Patrice went into the bedroom

much earlier than usual and lay in bed, staring up at the ceiling. At ten-thirty, Nefrititi staggered sleepily in and all but collapsed on her bed, going to sleep immediately. Then, at one-thirty, Patrice awoke to find Cherise tiptoeing around the room, preparing for bed.

"What are you doing here?" Patrice asked groggily.

"Girl, I wasn't up to dealing with anyone tonight. I figured I'd come here and crash. Sometimes I don't feel like being bothered, you know," answered Cherise through her pajama shirt, which was currently over her head.

Silently, Patrice watched her sister struggle to get her head through the appropriate hole, which seemed to be very difficult for her. After a few moments of fighting and wrestling with the shirt, Cherise yanked it off and threw it on the floor.

"Are you okay?" asked Patrice as her sister pulled another pajama shirt out of her drawer.

"Yeah, a bit drunk, I guess. Can't get my clothes on."

"I see," replied Patrice as Cherise got that shirt on, inside out and backward.

Cherise stumbled out of the room and Patrice could hear her in the bathroom, throwing up.

A few minutes later, Cherise came in looking a bit more sober. Her clothes had been fixed and her face washed free of makeup.

"Cherise, do you think I can borrow thirty dollars? I'll pay you back as soon as possible," blurted Patrice. She hadn't meant to ask, but she couldn't seem to stop it from coming out.

Cherise sighed heavily. "What you need thirty dollars for?"

"The application for Dogwood," Patrice answered, not quite honestly. She figured that if she told Cherise that she needed it to go see their mother, Cherise would just say that she would drive her down there. Then Cherise would never get around to it, and Patrice could kiss all chances of going to Dogwood Academy goodbye.

"You ask Aunt Mae?"

"No, I don't like asking her for money. She is always sending money to our mom and she's kept me for all this time. I don't feel right asking her to give me more."

Cherise nodded. "Yeah, you right. Okay, but it will have to be after this week. I almost got enough money saved for the first and last month's rent on this apartment I want. I should have that by the end of the week. Then I'll get you the money. But you *will* pay me back."

"Yes! Thank you, Cherise! Thank you so much. I promise to get the money to you. Grandma sends me five dollars for Easter and then twenty dollars for my birthday in May. Then maybe this summer I can work at the beauty shop sweeping or something and get you the rest.

Or maybe you could pay me for doing all your chores around here."

"Aw, that's cold, sis. Whatever. Good night, Patrice."

"Good night, Cherise."

Patrice smiled softly to herself in the dark. Maybe Monty was right. Maybe it would all work out, after all.

13

THE NEXT WEEK went by without much excitement. Patrice was getting used to the kind of attention that Monty paid to her, as was the rest of the eighth grade. Even Chanterelle, Sarah, and Raven had grown tired of trying to figure out the nature of Patrice and Monty's relationship. As for Eddie and Rasheed, they had reappeared at school, and Patrice made a point of giving them a wide berth. Whenever she saw them, they gave her the dirtiest, nastiest looks she'd ever seen, but only if she wasn't with Monty. If Monty was beside her, they ignored Patrice. And while she felt safe as long as Monty was around, she worried that if given the chance, they would get back at her for causing them trouble.

Patrice had learned that they had been taken down to

the police station. Because it was their first offense, they hadn't been charged or arrested, but they did have to take classes every Saturday morning for the next six months on managing anger. Patrice hoped fervently that the classes would work.

The tutoring that Patrice was giving Michael was going well. He appeared more confident about his reading and his numbers. Although he was still behind compared to Nefrititi, Patrice felt that by the end of the year they'd be neck and neck.

Patrice was extremely curious about Monty's grades, but didn't have the nerve to ask him how school was going. They were due for a progress report on February 10 and she was dying to know what his would look like. On Wednesday, Patrice had poked her head into the principal's office looking for Mrs. Hutton. It had been a week since she'd given her the essays and she was hoping to get some feedback and work on them over the weekend. Mrs. Hutton hadn't been available and Patrice had walked away disappointed.

On Friday, after the last bell, Mrs. Hutton had found Patrice in the hall and pulled her aside. "You are quite a gifted writer, Patrice," she had said, beaming. "The essays are wonderful. They are ready to go."

She reminded Patrice about the parental consent, as if Patrice didn't think about that constantly. Mrs. Hutton said she was anxious to turn in the entire application.

She seemed sure that Patrice would win one of the scholarships. Patrice was hopeful now, too, until she made the mistake of asking Mrs. Hutton how many students were applying for it.

"Oh, I'd say about a hundred kids or so in Chicago."

After seeing the horrified look on Patrice's face, she had quickly added, "But I'm willing to bet that only half of those kids will have the grades you have, and only half of *them* can write as well as you can. So I bet there are only about twenty-five or so kids you're competing with."

Twenty-five kids! For some reason, Patrice had thought that only a dozen kids would be applying for the three scholarships. After hearing that number, she wasn't so confident. Then, to make matters worse, she happened to turn down the hallway to find Eddie and Rasheed wandering around. She stopped short in her tracks. She could hear their snickering and laughter as she turned and walked the opposite way. Patrice did not know whether their classes were helping, but she was in no mood to find out.

Unfortunately, Monty wasn't anywhere in sight. He was usually waiting for her at her locker at the end of the day. Patrice hurriedly put on her coat and grabbed her bag, looking over her shoulder for Eddie and Rasheed, or for Monty. Seeing no one, she ran to the door and left the school.

Patrice walked quickly toward home, then had a change of heart and turned in the direction of her sister's beauty shop.

Walking into the Cut'n'Style always intimidated Patrice. Maybe it was the loud, boisterous stylists, who wanted to know why she didn't come in on a regular basis to get her hair done. Or maybe it was the glamorous customers. Whatever it was, Patrice rarely came into the shop and generally caused a major scene when she did. Today was no different.

"Hey! Look who has graced us with her presence!" shouted the owner from behind the front desk.

"Hello, Mercedes," said Patrice politely.

"Yo, Cherise! Your mysterious little sister is here," said Judea, the stylist nearest the front.

"Hey, girl!" called Cherise. "Come on back. What you doing here?"

Patrice walked over to Cherise, who was sitting in her own chair.

"Hi, Cherise. Where's your customer?"

"Girl, that old bag canceled on me at the last minute. Don't think I won't be charging her a cancellation fee next time I see her, ole trifling heifer. I was supposed to be braiding her hair. I could have booked at least three other appointments. I can't stand her. Geez, 'Trice, look at your hair. That funky ponytail is back. Sit down."

Patrice sat down obediently. Cherise put a cape on her, and told her to head to the sinks.

Cherise expertly shampooed and conditioned Patrice's hair and began blowing it dry. Patrice was so stunned by this free hair styling that she felt bad about bringing up the thirty dollars she had come by hoping to collect. She was building up her nerve when Judea asked Cherise about her new apartment.

"Girl, shoot, that old bag who canceled messed me up. I was this close to having all the money I needed, then she dogged me out."

"Cherise, you did about ten heads yesterday, and then another four this morning. Why you got to depend on Ms. Breeze for the down payment?"

" 'Cause we went out on Wednesday and I spent too much money on them Fuzzy Navel drinks we were having. Plus, then we went to breakfast on Thursday. And them boots I been wanting finally went on sale. Now I ain't got as much as I thought I'd have."

Well, thought Patrice. *That's that*. She fought to keep her face neutral.

As if reading her mind, Cherise looked at her through the mirror. "Hey, little sis," said Cherise. "Don't freak. I didn't forget the money I'm gonna loan you. I will have to get you that money next Friday, 'kay? I've got two reliable braid appointments, plus two colors next week. I should be rolling in money by then. Promise."

Patrice smiled. She hadn't forgotten!

"Sure, Cherise, whatever works for you."

"Now, Patrice," lectured Judea, "the next time you come in here, I want your hair to look exactly like that. Don't be coming in this shop with that beautiful hair of yours in another sad-looking ponytail."

This time Patrice's hair fell back magically off her face straight and smooth, curling softly at the ends.

"Whoa," Patrice said. "I'll never be able to make it look like this!"

Cherise and Judea laughed.

"Good thing you cain't. If people could do their hair like this, we'd be out of business," said Judea.

"Girl, you know that's right!"

Cherise and Judea high-fived each other while Patrice smiled and thanked her sister profusely.

She walked home, glad that for once the wind wasn't blowing. She didn't want her hair to get messed up. As she was strolling along, she realized how dark it was getting. It was Friday and she was supposed to watch Nefrititi and MarcAnthony. She groaned. She had totally lost track of time in her surprise and delight at getting her hair done. Auntie Mae would be long gone by now, and the kids alone. She ran the rest of the way home and arrived at the apartment panicked and out of breath.

When she hurried into the apartment, Monty and

Michael were playing Uno and watching cartoons with Nefrititi and MarcAnthony.

"Hey, we've been waiting for you," said Michael, going up to Patrice.

"You have? I'm sorry to make you wait. My aunt let you in?"

"Well, yeah," said Monty. "Then she had to go in to work and no one knew where you were. I got the feeling that she really needed to leave, so I offered to babysit. I guess she was feeling desperate."

Patrice groaned. She'd been thinking so much about herself and her needs that she had forgotten all about getting home for her aunt. For the first time, she could understand how Cherise seemed to forget about others.

"I can't believe I totally spaced out like that. I've never done it before. I feel terrible."

Monty, who was walking around Patrice in circles, examining her hair, grinned. "Hey, it was definitely worth the wait."

14

THE MONTH OF FEBRUARY started and the Chicago winter seemed to be digging in its heels. The weather stayed cold. The skies were gray. Life at school had settled into a routine. The gang of boys Monty used to lead seemed to be fracturing. On Monday, at lunch, for the first time Patrice could remember, they didn't all sit together. Monty ate lunch with her now, while a couple of the boys had begun to spend more and more time hanging around with Raven, Sarah, and Chanterelle. A few times Rasheed and Eddie disappeared at lunch, sometimes sneaking back into the cafeteria right before the bell, sometimes not. Patrice cheered to herself whenever they were gone for the rest of the day.

The tutoring sessions continued, as well. The homework group had a little celebration on Wednesday when Michael had completed a whole page of addition and subtraction problems without missing a single one.

The next thing Patrice knew, it was Friday. She felt jittery and nervous. Each time she heard the elevator door ding in the distance, her heart would flip. As the time passed with no sign of Cherise or the promised thirty dollars, Patrice became more anxious.

Finally, Monty, who of course was there with Michael, couldn't take her fidgeting any longer. It wasn't like her.

"What is up with you?" he asked after she had jumped up and peered out of the peephole for what seemed like the thousandth time. "What is your deal?"

Patrice sat down at the dining room table and looked at her hands. She shrugged and hoped he would drop it.

Monty, being Monty, wasn't satisfied with that tactic. "That don't tell me nothing, 'Trice." He left the board game he was playing with Nefrititi, MarcAnthony, and Michael and joined Patrice at the table.

She continued to look at her hands, but could feel his eyes on her. She sighed and looked up into them.

Sometimes she wondered if a lot of what Monty felt for her was pity. It was a little nagging feeling she got, and although he had never said anything to make her think that way, she wanted to make sure that she didn't give him any reason to feel sorry for her.

"I'm waiting for my sister. She's supposed to be bringing me the thirty dollars I need," she answered. "I keep thinking that she'll space me out."

This time it was Monty who shrugged. "Is that it? I told you it would all work out."

Patrice smiled weakly at him, hoping that he was right. The rest of the night passed uneventfully: Monty and Michael eventually left, Nefrititi and MarcAnthony eventually went to bed, and Aunt Mae eventually came home. Cherise never appeared.

One more week, thought Patrice. Next Friday was Valentine's Day, and if she didn't get the money by then, Dogwood Academy was history.

• • •

Progress reports were handed out on Monday. As usual, Patrice had gotten straight A's, with remarks on her good behavior from her teachers. She was dying to know what Monty's progress report looked like, and as she waited for him to get his coat on, she was thinking about how she could ask him when Mrs. Hutton appeared and invited them both to her office.

Patrice groaned inwardly. She knew that Mrs. Hutton would ask for the application form. Time was almost up. She didn't want to explain to Mrs. Hutton what she had to do to get her mother to sign it. A trip to prison wasn't something to brag about. To Patrice it felt like a dirty little secret, and she did not want everyone to know about it.

As expected, Mrs. Hutton opened the conversation by asking Patrice if she had gotten her application form signed yet. Patrice hemmed and hawed and gave her an answer that clearly did not satisfy Mrs. Hutton.

"I'm not sure what the problem is, but if there is something I can do to help, let me know. I need all your materials by the eighteenth. No extensions."

Patrice nodded, her face feeling hot.

"Yes, ma'am, I know. I'm taking care of it myself. I have it under control," she answered, feeling as if she had nothing at all under control.

She was glad when Mrs. Hutton turned to Monty and said, "Mr. Freeman, I've seen your latest progress report and I have to say I am flabbergasted."

Monty scowled. "Yeah, what about it?" he snapped.

Patrice glanced at him, silently willing him to be less disrespectful. Mrs. Hutton's eyebrow shot up at his tone, but she did not seem unduly offended.

"In my twenty years of teaching and my ten years of being a principal here, I have never seen such astounding improvement in a student in such a short time. It's quite remarkable, really."

Patrice grinned and looked at Monty. She felt an overwhelming urge to hug him.

Monty's scowl faded. His face went through several

different expressions before settling on one which was a mixture of pride and surprise. "No joke?" he said, his tone markedly different from the one he had just used.

"Yes, no joke," replied Mrs. Hutton with a smile. "I, quite frankly, am without words. I only hope whatever you are doing is something that you continue to do. Your standardized test scores have always been high. I pulled your scores and there is only one student who has consistently scored higher than you have on those tests, and she's sitting next to you."

It was now Patrice's face that held a mixture of surprise and pride. Monty smiled at her.

"To be honest, your poor grades and your behavior have always been a great source of disappointment, Mr. Freeman. That is, until now. What you have done in such a short period of time is miraculous. I expect you to further improve your grades. I know you are capable of more than the straight B's you received."

"Straight B's!" cried Monty. "No joke?"

"Yes, Monty, no joke. And by the end of the year, I expect you to have the straight A's that your friend here has," she said with a gesture toward Patrice. "Then next year I will be telling your high school principal to give you an application for the Dogwood Academy scholarship. That's a promise."

"Yes, ma'am," replied Monty, trying hard to regain his usual composure.

As they stood to leave, Mrs. Hutton called to Patrice, "I need that permission form, Patrice."

Patrice simply nodded. This coming weekend was her last chance to get to her mother. She was officially out of time.

15

ALL WEEK Patrice waited patiently for Cherise to appear with the money. The rest of Monday went by without her coming, as did Tuesday and Wednesday. By Thursday night, Patrice decided that Cherise must have forgotten about it because she hadn't called or come by in days. So Friday, after school, Patrice left Monty talking with his math teacher, cast aside her pride, and quickly walked again to the beauty shop. She hadn't wanted to nag Cherise about the money, but she was too anxious now to wait for her sister to show up. Keeping an eye on the time so she wouldn't leave Auntie Mae in the lurch again, she hurriedly pushed open the door to the shop.

"Yo, I don't believe it. Twice in one month," teased Mercedes.

Patrice smiled and started heading toward the back.

"Um, excuse me, Miss Brain, but Girlfriend ain't here."

Patrice's stomach did a flip. "Do you think she'll be back soon?"

"Girl, no. She got finished early and then some fine dark-chocolate man came in and picked her up. I don't expect to see her till tomorrow."

"Tomorrow?" repeated Patrice softly. *Oh dear*, she thought, *this can't be good*. "Well, thank you, Mercedes. If you see her tonight, would you please ask her to call me at home?"

"Sure thing, honey, but as fine as that man was, I don't expect to see her hanging out at no club tonight! She left here with a oversized Valentine's bear in one arm and that chocolate cutie-pie on the other."

Patrice nodded weakly and walked out of the shop to the sound of catcalls and hollers from the other stylists discussing Cherise's latest conquest.

All the way home, Patrice told herself over and over again not to worry. After all, she couldn't expect other girls, especially girls like Cherise, to ignore Valentine's Day the way she did. Deep down she had hoped for something from Monty, but considering that he sometimes didn't have food in his house, she hadn't gotten her hopes too high. It was a good thing, because she hadn't received a pink carnation or a red lollipop.

Besides, she had more important things to worry about today than cheap flowers and candy, such as getting money from Cherise. As she walked home, she told herself that Cherise would be at the shop tomorrow morning, and all she would have to do was leave the apartment earlier than she had planned to give herself enough time to walk to the beauty shop before heading over to the bus station. The shop was pretty much on the way to the bus, so it wasn't as if it was going to take all that long.

• • •

For the second time, Patrice stayed up late Friday night getting her weekend chores done. Saturday morning she headed out the door half an hour earlier than she had on the day of her first visit to her mother.

Patrice walked quickly to the beauty parlor, trying to ignore the sick feeling in the pit of her stomach when she noticed that Cherise's car was nowhere in sight. To quell the panic rising in her, she reasoned that the dark-chocolate man had picked her up, so maybe he had dropped her off, too.

Mercedes sat behind the desk, her head in her hands, looking cranky. "Hey, girl," she said without a trace of her usual sass. "She ain't here."

Patrice felt as if she'd been hit in the gut. "Do you know when she will be in?" she asked, trying to keep her voice from shaking.

"Not until Tuesday morning. She and Mr. Fine went to the concert last night and really hit it off, so she had me cancel a couple of her customers, and traded the rest to the other stylists. Since Mr. Fine has Monday off, I guess they decided to drive to Joliet and spend the weekend on one of them riverboat casinos. She's smart, though; I should have done the same thing. I'm too hungover to function."

Patrice felt numb. She couldn't even respond. She nodded and walked out of the door.

No Cherise, no money. No money, no bus ticket. No bus ticket, no signature. No signature, no chance for a scholarship. There was no chance that Patrice wouldn't burst into tears. And she did, just as Monty appeared.

"Hey, girl, whoa. What is going on? I saw you leaving the building all early. You come here to cry?" he joked.

Patrice shook her head. She couldn't begin to try and talk. She just kept crying.

"Patrice, tell me what's wrong," Monty said. "Come here. Calm down."

Monty led her over to a nearby bus bench. He pulled out an old Kentucky Fried Chicken napkin from his jacket and handed it to her.

Patrice used it wipe her eyes and blow her nose. Then she turned to him with sad eyes. The sobbing had stopped, but her tears continued to flow. "She's not there," she said simply, as if that explained everything.

"Who? Cherise? So what, your hair is great," Monty replied. "It's pretty, really it is."

Patrice shook her head and sighed. "Remember, Cherise was supposed to lend me thirty dollars so I could take the bus to see my mother so she could sign the application," Patrice explained with a shaky voice.

"Oh! Well, go next week. Leave Cherise a note or something," suggested Monty.

Patrice shook her head again, her tears flowing even quicker.

"Next week will be too late. You heard Mrs. Hutton yesterday! The application is due on the eighteenth." Patrice knew she was whining, but she couldn't help it. "If I don't get to my mom, then I can forget about Dogwood."

"Okay. Well, when *is* Cherise going to be here?" Monty said calmly.

"Tuesday!" wailed Patrice.

"Oh, that is a problem."

"It's over. Just forget it. I don't care!" shouted Patrice.

Monty looked at her, then at his watch. "Okay. Okay. Wait here. Don't move," he commanded. "I'll fix this."

Patrice shrugged. She slumped back onto the bench and let the tears roll down her cheeks unchecked. Now that her dream was shattered, she admitted to herself how much she had wanted to win one of those scholarships. She had wanted to leave Chicago, even though it meant that she would have to leave Monty. She had wanted to leave her aunt's apartment, to leave the endless chores, the cold, the wind. There was no guarantee that she would have gotten one of the scholarships, but she had wanted to try. Now she was trapped here in a place where she would never feel comfortable.

Patrice didn't know exactly how long she had been sitting at that cold bus stop crying, but all of a sudden, she felt a hand on her wrist pulling her to her feet.

"Come on, Patrice, we gotta hurry!" said Monty, snatching her backpack and pulling her forward. "Come, girl, move, move!"

Monty was in a full sprint, dragging Patrice next to him. It was all she could do to keep up. She ran headlong into the street, gasping as Monty barely missed getting them creamed by a police car, siren blaring, heading in the direction they had just come from.

"Whoa, that was close! Come on, Patrice! Come on!"

Running down the street, she followed at Monty's heels as he expertly wove in and out of the Saturday morning crowd. The police siren faded.

"Where are we going?" Patrice shouted at Monty's back.

"Don't talk, 'Trice. Run!" he yelled over his shoulder.

They ran full speed for what seemed like forever. She followed Monty into the bus station and up to the counter.

"Two round-trip tickets to Joliet," Monty said to the clerk. He pulled a wad of cash out of his pocket.

"That will be forty-eight dollars," said the clerk, sliding two tickets to Monty. "You had better hurry. The bus is about to leave."

"Yo, thanks, man. Come on!"

Monty sprinted toward the bus.

Patrice ran after him. "Monty! Wait! Monty!" she yelled.

"Girl, come on!"

Monty and Patrice got onto the bus and dropped clumsily into their seats, huffing and puffing as the bus pulled off.

"Hey, girl, you can run. If you get dumb all of a sudden, you can try for a track scholarship."

"I can't believe it. How did you get the money? I'll pay you back, I promise. I can't believe I'm going! And you're coming with me!" Patrice said between pants.

She suddenly felt extremely happy. Giddy even. She turned to Monty and grinned. "I can't believe you did this for me!" she said.

Monty looked at her and shrugged. "It's no biggie. I didn't have anything else to do today. Consider it a late Valentine's Day gift."

"You are wonderful. You are the best thing in my life!" she declared, and before she knew what she was doing, she leaned over and gave him a soft kiss. Right on the lips.

"Oh." She looked away. "Thanks, Monty. Thank you so much," she said to the window, too embarrassed to actually look at him. "How can I ever repay you?"

"You just did, Patrice," he said. "You just did."

· · ·

After they caught their breath, they fell into a companionable silence. Patrice looked idly out the window as the bus roared toward Joliet, out of the city, into the suburbs, and then past hundreds of fallow cornfields.

Then, out of nowhere, a tiny voice in the back of her head asked, *Where did he get all that money?* It had happened so quickly. Where had he gone so suddenly? And what had he done? He had a wad of money, more than the twenty-four dollars apiece it took to get them both to Joliet. She had seen that when he peeled off three twenties for the tickets. He must have had at least one hundred dollars in that wad, probably even a little more than that. Where had he gotten so much money so fast?

Patrice thought back to the scene at the bus stop. She had been so upset that she hadn't noticed where he had gone. She also had no idea how long he had been gone. Surely that police siren hadn't been for him.

She looked at him. "Monty?"

"Yo."

"How did you do this? I mean, this trip is going to be pretty expensive for you."

Monty shrugged.

"It's just that . . ." She wasn't sure how she should phrase this question.

Monty looked at her and smirked. "What is it, Patrice?"

Patrice felt her face getting hot. "I was curious about how you got so much money so quick, that's all."

Monty stared at her, then shrugged nonchalantly. "Don't worry about it."

"It's so much money, though, Monty."

"Patrice. Don't stress about it. No biggie. 'Kay?"

· · ·

In Joliet, as they were waiting for the bus to take them to the prison, Monty suddenly turned to Patrice. "You bring your moms anything?"

Patrice shook her head. All she had with her were the forms that she needed her mother to sign.

"Wait here." Monty started to walk across the street.

"Monty!" yelled Patrice. "The bus will be here soon!"

Monty threw up a hand in acknowledgment and started to run. He disappeared around the corner. Patrice had the four dollars from the last trip with her, enough to get to the prison and back, but she didn't want to leave without Monty.

A few minutes passed. Patrice was pacing by the bus stop, looking first in the direction from which the bus would be coming, then back in the direction in which Monty had run. As she feared, the bus appeared before Monty. *Oh no.*

Just as the bus approached the intersection, for the second time that day she heard police sirens. The bus screeched to a halt, letting the police car pass, and then the light turned red, forcing the bus to wait. Patrice watched as the police cruiser sped past her down the street and around the same corner that Monty had turned. As the car turned, Monty came sprinting up the street, stopping himself from darting in front of the cruiser. After it had passed, he ran back to the bus stop, a paper bag clutched in his hand.

"Did we miss it?" he said between huffs of breath. "Did the bus come?"

Patrice shook her head numbly. She didn't know what to think. What was going on? The light changed, the bus pulled up, and Monty paid for both of them. Surely there wasn't a connection between the police cars and Monty.

Around twelve-thirty they were in the chilly, beige prison waiting room. Monty flopped down on one of the seats and waited as Patrice carefully filled out the form, this time without leaving blank spaces. After handing it to the same surly guard as before, Patrice sat next to Monty, fidgeting with the application form she held in her sweaty hands.

"Chill, girl. Everything will be fine. You don't really got to say nothing more to her than 'Sign this form' and 'See ya later.' "

Patrice nodded, too nervous to reply.

"Patrice Williams!"

The sound of her name made her jump nervously to her feet. Monty snatched a sports magazine out of the paper bag and then shoved the bag at Patrice.

"Give this to your moms," he said.

She took it without thinking. Her stomach was full of butterflies.

"Follow me, please."

With a parting glance back at Monty, who gave her a wink and a smile, she followed the guard through the door.

16

THE GUARD LED PATRICE down a maze of beige hallways to a room filled with a bunch of circular tables, many of which were already taken. She left Patrice standing at the entrance.

Patrice looked around. Suddenly she saw her mother. She walked slowly to the table at which her mother sat smoking a cigarette.

"Hi, Mom."

"Well, well, well. Look at little Patrice," her mother said, surveying her. "All grown up."

Patrice examined her mother, too. She looked much older than she had just a year ago. Her hair, so beautiful when she had come to get Patrice at her grandmother's, was now pulled into a sloppy ponytail and streaked with gray. Her teeth looked in need of a cleaning and were stained yellow. Her eyes seemed dull and her skin dry.

They looked at each other silently for a few minutes.

"Well, what you want? You came down here to see me, I didn't send for you," remarked her mother, sitting back in the chair and dragging the last puff from her cigarette. "Did you bring me something?" She gestured toward Patrice's hands.

"Oh, yes, ma'am," said Patrice. "I need you to sign these papers for me. For that scholarship contest I wrote about in the letter."

Patrice held out the forms. Her mother glanced at them, but didn't reach out. Her eyes shifted back to the paper bag that Patrice still held.

"Uh-uh. I was talking about what's in that sack. Did you bring *me* something?"

"Oh, yeah. Sorry. Here."

Patrice reached into the bag and grabbed the first thing that her hand fell on and slid it over to her mother.

"Now, that's what I'm talking about. A box of cigarettes." Patrice's mother looked appreciatively at the present Monty had bought.

Patrice pulled a pen out of her backpack and set it on the table. "Mom, could you sign the forms for me, please?"

"Yeah, whatever. Give 'em here."

Patrice pushed the papers toward her mother and waited. Her mother simply looked at them and then back at her. "Well, you got a pen?"

"It's right there." Patrice heard the irritation in her own voice, but she didn't care. She rolled the pen closer to her mother.

Her mother signed the papers, wrote her social security number in the appropriate box, and shoved the papers back at Patrice.

It was done! Finally! Patrice sat smiling at the papers. She looked up at her mother. "Thank you so much, Mom! This school is great! It has—"

Her mother waved her comments away. "You bring me anything else?"

"Excuse me?"

"That bag you got. Did you bring me something else?"

Patrice looked at the paper bag. As her mother evidently had noticed, it didn't seem empty. She reached in and pulled out about ten Hershey bars.

"Yeah, these will work. Not bad, not bad. You pretty smart for a country girl."

Patrice nodded absentmindedly. How on earth had Monty been able to buy a carton of cigarettes? He certainly didn't look old enough to get them without trouble. A vision of the police car racing in the same direction that Monty had come running from flashed in her mind.

The thought that he cared enough about Patrice to risk getting into trouble brought another thought into Patrice's head: she realized that someone did care about her and it wasn't the woman sitting across from her.

"Girl, that is great. Come here, baby, give your mama a kiss."

Patrice blinked her eyes, trying to refocus.

"Come on over here and give your mama a kiss."

Patrice didn't move. She wasn't remotely interested in showing any affection to this stranger. And for once she had the internal strength not to do just as she was told. Pleasing this woman was not important to her.

"Why did you take me away from Grandma?" Patrice blurted out.

Her mother dropped her outstretched arms and gave Patrice a look that made her wish she hadn't asked.

"Girl, you my child. You needed to be with me."

Patrice snorted derisively. "Yes, Mom, that worked real well, didn't it? I mean, we were together for what? Eight weeks?"

"Girl, don't you talk to me like that. I'm your mama."

Patrice started to say she was sorry, but when she opened her mouth, different words tumbled out. Not words from her mind, but words that seemed to come straight from the deep pool of anger that she had been ignoring for a year.

"I was happy with Grandma. I was cared for. You

never cared for or about me, Mom. I wish you had left me alone. You only came for me to try and get yourself out of trouble."

"Watch your mouth, little girl. You so ungrateful. You living in Chicago now. A big city. You would have been countrified had you stayed in that little hick town." Her mother had already opened the carton and taken out a pack of cigarettes. She was patting the pockets on her bright orange jumper, obviously looking for matches. "How is your grandma anyway?"

"She's fine. She lives in a nursing home now."

"See. You couldn't have stayed with her. You would have been nothing but a burden to her."

Patrice stared at her mother. Within her something settled, solidified. She stood to go.

"Sit down, girl. We got till one forty-five!"

Patrice continued to gather her papers. She didn't want to stay. She had what she needed now and all she wanted to do was get back to Monty. To be with someone who acted as if she was important.

"Goodbye, Mother."

"Girl, sit down. You go now, I got to go back to my cell. I'm enjoying this little outing. Sit down and tell me some gossip. How is Cherise and Marquis? Give me some news."

Patrice remained standing. "Cherise is fine. She still

works at the Cut'n'Style and is moving out of Auntie Mae's apartment. I have no idea how Marquis is; I spent even less time with him than I did with you. And I don't have any gossip for you. I wrote everything I knew in the letter. I'm leaving now. Thank you again for signing the papers."

"Sit down, Patrice. Don't you want to talk some more?"

Patrice remembered Monty's words: *You don't really got to say nothing more to her than "Sign this form" and "See ya later."*

Patrice stared directly into her mother's eyes and simply said, "No. No, I don't. See ya later."

With that, she turned and walked out of the room. The guard took her visitor's badge and pointed her toward the waiting room. Patrice never looked back.

• • •

She found Monty stretched across a couple of chairs in the waiting room, reading the magazine that he had bought at the store along with the cigarettes and candy bars. He looked up at her, obviously surprised to see her so quickly.

Patrice strolled over to the seats and sat next to Monty, who sat up and watched her carefully.

"You okay? You get them papers signed?"

Patrice smiled wanly. "Yes, they're signed." Just saying those words gave warmth to her smile.

"You didn't stay long to talk with her."

Patrice looked at him and felt the usual heat behind her eyes that told her she was about to cry. She swallowed and took a deep breath. The heat abated. She looked at Monty and shrugged. She would not cry about this, not about her mother. Besides, she was tired of crying, sick of feeling tears dribble down her cheeks.

"No. I hate that she's in there, but it's no one's fault but her own. I mean, she wasn't even interested in what I was doing."

Monty nodded.

"We talked enough for me to know that I don't need to talk with her again. Ever."

"Ever? That's a pretty long time, 'Trice," Monty replied softly.

Monty looked at Patrice. He appeared to be bracing himself for an onslaught of tears, but even though she felt as if she could start weeping at any moment, she also felt less delicate, more in control.

"Well, maybe next year or something. I'm so mad at her for—well, for everything. I think I need time to forgive her for what she's done."

"Patrice, are you going to be okay?"

Patrice turned to Monty, leaned forward, and kissed him on the lips—this time without feeling shy. "Yes, I am. Thank you, Monty. Thank you for caring about me. Come on. Let's head back into town."

Monty, for once, was the speechless one.

They stood outside the prison walls, shivering in the cold while waiting for the bus to come. Patrice was quiet on the bus ride, while Monty seemed to be trying to regain his typical cool after getting that second kiss.

On reaching Joliet, Patrice realized that in her haste to leave her mother, she hadn't remembered that the bus to Chicago didn't leave for hours.

"When does the bus come?" Monty asked, settling himself on the bench in the shabby bus station.

Patrice looked at him sheepishly. "Six thirty-five," she answered quietly.

"Six thirty-five!" Monty yelped, sitting straight up. "What time is it?"

"I don't really know. What does your fancy watch say?" she asked, trying to keep the conversation light.

Monty looked at her, then shrugged.

"I'm sorry about this, Monty. I know it's a long wait. Really, though, what time is it? Exactly how long do we have to be here?"

Monty shrugged again. "Don't matter, do it? Bus comes at six thirty-five no matter what time it is now."

"I know. I'll make all this up to you somehow, Monty, I promise. Seriously, though, how long do we have to wait?"

Monty waved her off and tugged at the arm of his jacket. "I ain't got my watch."

"Yes, you do! When we were sitting on the bench in front of the beauty shop, you looked at it. Right before you ran—"

Patrice stopped mid-sentence. Her eyes grew wide as all the pieces fell into place. "Monty," she whispered. "You didn't."

Monty glanced at her face before tugging again at the arm of his jacket. "What?"

"Oh my God, Monty," she moaned. "He gave that to you!"

Patrice reached over to Monty and yanked his coat sleeve up. Just as she had guessed, his wrist was empty. His fancy watch was gone. "You sold your watch. That's where you got all that money from. Geez, Monty!" Patrice sat down heavily on the bench. Her hands covered her mouth. Her eyes were wide in disbelief. "Monty. Your watch. It was such a nice watch. I can't believe you sold it."

"It's not that big a deal, Patrice. Really."

But to Patrice it was a really big deal. He had taken the one thing of value that he owned and sold it for her. At the same time, she had been scared that he'd robbed a store to get the money they were using. She slowly shook her head back and forth, not sure which surprised her more.

"Patrice, stop bugging. It's no big deal. I ain't seen that man for years. You mean more to me than some watch from someone I don't even know."

Patrice looked at him. And for the third time that day, she kissed him.

17

SINCE MONDAY WAS PRESIDENT'S DAY, Patrice turned in the completed application to Mrs. Hutton first thing Tuesday morning. Now all she had to do was wait.

Life settled into a pleasant routine. Homework on Mondays, Wednesdays, and Fridays was still done at Auntie Mae's dining room table—MarcAnthony, Nefrititi, and Michael had become fast friends. Michael had become more sure of himself. He talked and laughed often. His crush on Nefrititi was now glaringly obvious, especially to Nefrititi, with whom Patrice had to have more than one conversation about not treating him like her servant.

Monty's grades were getting closer to Patrice's. He hadn't gotten straight A's yet, but he was almost there.

Monty's group had all but fallen apart. It seemed that without Monty at its core, there was no one to keep the different personalities together. Rasheed had disappeared. Rumor had it that he had gotten into trouble again and been sent to the same home that Marquis was in. Eddie, without his partner, was far less bold. He still teased Patrice, but she no longer feared him. More than once she had been able to answer his comments with such sharp retorts of her own that he had stopped dead in his tracks. Of course, she was with Monty most of the time, but she no longer needed his protection from anyone.

By the beginning of March, it was clear that spring was coming. The city was very slowly melting. The sky turned from steel gray to light blue. Although anxious to hear about the scholarship, Patrice no longer saw it as her only hope. Now it was merely an option, one that she would love to have, but not one that was vital to her happiness.

On the first official day of spring, Mrs. Hutton pulled Patrice from her geometry class. Patrice felt her stomach clench, but she knew that she would not be heartbroken if she hadn't won.

Mrs. Hutton's face gave away the secret immediately. She waved a letter in front of Patrice and enclosed her in a big hug. "You did it! You did it!"

"The scholarship? I got one?"

"Yes! I knew you could do it!"

A huge grin on her face, Mrs. Hutton handed Patrice a letter that began:

Dear Miss Williams:
Congratulations! We are pleased to inform you that you have won one of the three . . .

Patrice read the letter five times on the walk home with Monty. She had Monty holding her left hand, the letter in her right hand, and the warm spring wind of Chicago against her back, pushing her forward.